A CHILD OF MAGIC

Christine Olivia Hernandez

SECOND EDITION

A CHILD OF MAGIC

First Published 2018

For those that see with eyes of heart—remember,

you are always children of magic

Acknowledgements

To Spencer Clem, my deepest heartfelt gratitude. Maltyox for taking the book to new heights with your passion for rewriting and helping me tell this story. Thank you for your loyalty and dedication. I am eternally thankful for our past and present—looking forward to our future creations to come.

Also, a thank you to all of the children of magic in my life—the sisters and brothers who have held the vision of this book and shared it with your communities, maltyox!

Table of Contents

Acknowledgements v

Introduction ix

Cacao Ceremony xiii

Discovering Mother Earth 1

Wide Open Wings 11

Lessons from the Sea 21

Sharing The Magic 28

The Fog of Disenchantment 46

Shadows Creep In 53

The Calling 71

Shifts and Synchronicities 76

Oasis of Remembrance 82

Clearing Out the Fog 94

Sacred Lands 102

Found at the Water's Edge 127

Challenged 132

Beginning Again... 139

Magic out of the Mundane 149

Working Within 159

Reviving the Necklace 165

Introduction

A Child of Magic was written in and as a ceremony. When I sat down to write, I created a ritual of drinking ceremonial cacao, allowing the energy of cacao to channel through me. This was a healing process within itself, because it allowed me to discover my inner child and create freely from that place. I hope for you to create your own healing experience with this book by setting your own sacred space. I encourage you to drink ceremonial cacao, sit in presence, and read with the eyes of the inner child. This will support your heart opening to experience deep healing.

If you are wanting to awaken your own magic, cacao will help you see the world with fresh eyes once again. In this way, cacao has been a catalyst throughout my life. It helped reopen my eyes and heart after I'd experienced many traumas and heartbreaks—especially aiding me after my father took his own life. By using cacao intentionally, I connected with my inner child, fathers essence, and ancestors. This allowed me to access the magic of my body and soul that is only available through true openness to willingly experience both the pain and joys of the heart.

We all have the opportunity to make choices that support our growth and healing. Most destructive behaviors in adulthood stem from a wounded inner child.[1] As we age, we discover how the power of choice leads us to decide what is truly supportive. Gentle plant medicines can help us heal and come home to our hearts. Furthermore, when we heal from within, we remember that we are all children of magic who seek self-acceptance, personal validation, and unconditional love. With the assistance of cacao, we can experience that we truly are our own healers—able to care for, hold, and heal the inner child, looking upon our future self with less fear and more excitement. The world is filled with adults who have a wounded child running amok inside and are disconnected from their hearts. This unbalance creates a war within, which is reflected to the outside world as well—and so we find ourselves waging war against ourselves and each other. This has now become our collective history and through recurrent conflicts and genocides, humanity exists

---

[1] https://cptsdfoundation.org/2020/07/13/the-wounded-inner-child/

Cacao Ceremony

A Cacao Ceremony is a sacred space and safe container that allows us to experience our heart opening, feel a deep connection, and release negative energy. In this state of openness, we can feel gratitude, joy, and of course, magic! Through this, we remember our connection to our truth, being whole and complete as we are. Here, we can activate and awaken to our powers, prayers, and unique purpose.

In a ceremony, we honor the cacao spirit, each of the directions, the elements, the ancestors, and the Mayan wisdom keepers of this medicine. We honor our connection to all things knowing that we are one with it all. By remembering this we receive the greatest gift—to be and feel vibrantly alive!

Cacao is a gentle yet powerful plant and it is invigorating, allowing for release of what no longer serves us. It opens passages of creative energy within our energetic, spiritual, and physical bodies. Sometimes tears or sweat may come, releasing blocked emotions that can finally flow freely.

Others may feel joy, bliss, excitement, deepened focus, or a desire to dance and sing. Cacao is not a psychedelic yet it is a psychoactive that can boost your mood and on a deeper level, open you up to being more energetically alive. One psychoactive property within cacao is anandamide, known as the bliss molecule, which opens us to feeling bliss and euphoria! Remember all expressions that come through are welcome. Allow yourself to open and feel whatever is on your heart and give thanks for all of the healing that is happening. Enjoy!

Ceremonial Cacao Recipe

Ingredients:

1. 1 oz of Ceremonial grade cacao, my favorite is at www.maltyoxmethod.com. (listen to your body to see if you prefer a smaller amount)
2. 6 oz of hot water
3. Cayenne and cinnamon to taste (optional to help increase blood circulation)
4. 1 tsp of a natural sweetener such as mesquite, monkfruit, or tocos (optional)
5. Warmed coconut milk (optional for a more frothy drink)

Directions:

- Chop the cacao into small pieces with a knife so it softens easily in hot water
- Heat water just before a boil. It should be too hot to touch but not yet boiling
- Add the cacao (1 oz/2 tbsp)
- Add sweetening and spices to taste
- Say a prayer before blending

- Blend all ingredients in a blender that is safe for hot liquids or whisk together in a pot over medium-high heat until frothy

Note: The cacao should be 100 percent organic. If this is your first time using it and you don't have ceremonial cacao, then you can try organic cacao nibs or cacao paste. Do not use conventional chocolate or powder. Cocoa powder is highly processed, which removes the bean's natural fat found in cacao butter. Through this processing, most of the living enzymes, healthy fats, and subtle energetic properties of cacao are destroyed, thus, conventional chocolates and cocoa powders do not contain the pure properties of the cacao plant.

Setting Sacred Space:

- Use blessing herbs such as cedar, sage, or copal to cleanse yourself and the space around you
- Listen to beautiful healing music or sing a sweet melody to yourself
- Give thanks to your spirit guides, spirit animals, ancestors, Mother Earth, and Great Spirit
- Take deep, cleansing breaths, grounding into Mother

Earth before working with the cacao

= Serve while warm, give thanks, set intentions, and experience life open hearted!

Disclaimer: Cacao is strong, bitter, and can be a laxative in higher doses. Those needing a dietary detox or those on a raw diet should take less the first time to see how it feels. Some may get nausea or a mild headache 5–6 hours later, so consider going easy at first. Don't work with ceremonial doses of cacao if you are taking antidepressants or have a serious heart condition. Ceremonial doses of cacao are also not recommended in cases of high blood pressure or epilepsy.

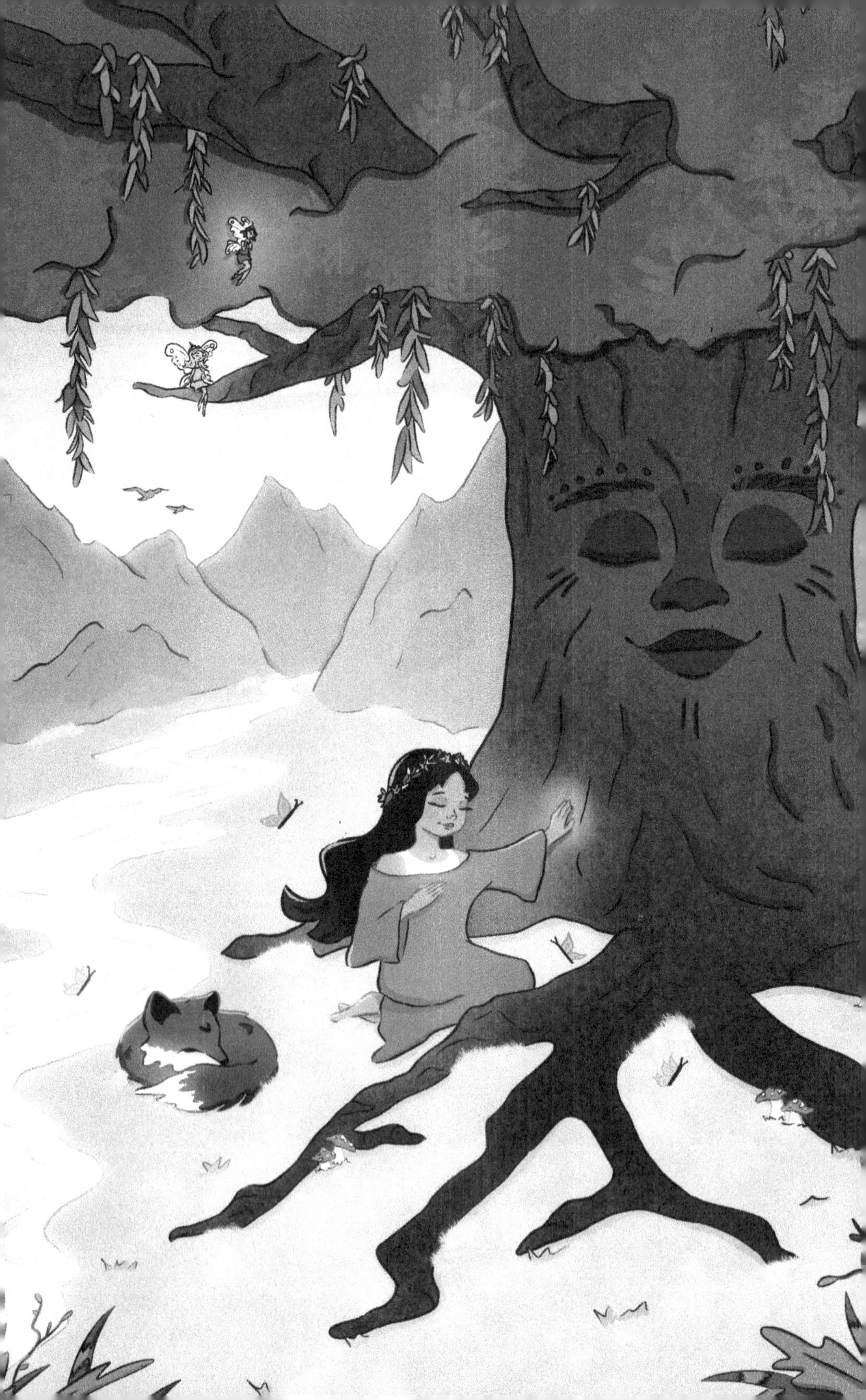

Discovering Mother Earth

One misty morning, Lana Livia was swinging in the park, imagining she was an eagle rising out of the smog and up into the clear sky. Like a mighty bird, she soared gracefully through the clouds, touching the sun with her glittering wings. Expressing her freedom with fluid movements and fearless measure, she left the gloomy city behind. As she flew, a familiar song beckoned from the direction of the forest, bringing her back into her body. Following the mystical music, she jumped off the swing and ran into the luscious greenery.

As Lana entered the woods, it transformed into an enchanted forest, alive with multicolored trees and flowers that fluttered to the music! Lana had discovered a haven for magic—a place where creatures like squirrels and deer could be playful and free, where butterflies danced and birds chirped along with the ancient oak's sweet melody. Amidst all of this beauty, she felt a deep connection to the oak tree and it's song was a loving invitation to reconnect with her truest nature.

Lana Livia was a child of magic, miraculous and extraordinary as ever a young spirit was. Made of pure love, she was sensitive and closely connected to her truth. Yet in moments of forgetfulness, her imagination helped her cope with an old world that didn't believe in magic.

Following her heart, as all children of magic do, Lana looked at the forest surrounding her in complete wonder. Two fairies flew above her head and danced towards the singing oak tree. They gifted her with a sylvan crown, wholly welcoming her to the forest. The fairies sang softly:

"We are loved, we are related in the light.

You are loved, you are the light.

Swing this way, let us remind you of your ways.

Sweet as the sun, Magic child we are one."

Bright-eyed with delight, she giggled and twirled, "Thank you," she exclaimed! Lana overflowed with so much joy and gratitude that the entire forest could feel it and glistened with pleasure. The fairies kissed her cheeks lightly and then introduced her to the singing tree.

"Oh how good for you to return, dear one!" The timeless

oak tree said, laughing with adoration. Her leaves stirred as her branches gently wove around Lana, in an adoring hug. "You have a wondrous imagination, and I delight in your connection to your truth and your magic."

"Wow! Thank you," Lana replied. "All of this is so beautiful, yet who are you?"

"You know who I am," the tree chuckled and said gently. "You simply forget that I am Mother Earth, Pachamama, Mama Gaia—whatever you would like to call me in this moment, dear child. I am part of you, as is this forest, and I am always here, whether you see me or not."

Lana realized she could faintly remember her. She liked the words the timeless oak spoke and she loved the whimsical way she felt when she said the name "*Pachamama*" aloud. She was beginning to remember.

"This is a truth that will soon be forgotten through your human experience," Pachamama told her. "You are only thinking about it now because at this time in your life, you are in the stages of forgetting. That is normal for your kind, yet you are the only child of magic who has dared to enter into the forest for many, many years. And so I say, you are here for a reason, and it is up to you to remember this truth. The world you were born into will try to keep you from remembering Lana, but in perfect timing, you will have all you need to return home to me—home to the magic."

Lana beamed with a glistening, golden aura that expanded deep into the forest. Feeling loved and inspired, she hugged the oak's trunk tightly. "Pachamama, I wish to hold onto my truth, I will try to remember this feeling forever."

Pachamama began to sing in a way that was otherworldly, like a mother singing a nursery rhyme to her infant. It was a language beyond words that conveyed the deepest love. Lana looked around at all the beauty surrounding her. Although she couldn't fully remember, Lana sensed she'd had many special moments here before. She couldn't recollect all the details, yet she felt a familiar comfort. She felt safe and more at home than ever before.

Pachamama said, "You are a child of magic and always will be."

Lana climbed up the ancient tree to the tiny nest of her beloved fairy friends; sisters Juniper and Marigold. She loved their beds made of blue moss, mushroom-cap pillows, and the tiny yellow flowers that decorated their living area. It was wonderful, and Lana did her best to memorize every magical detail so she could recreate it back at her own house. She sat with a broad smile on her face as the fairies brought over tiny translucent flowers filled with sweet nectar to sip. It was always such a delicious treat!

"I've had this before, haven't I?" Lana asked. "I remember this taste. It's so flavorful," she said, savoring the sweet floral essence.

"It's your favorite," said Juniper, sparkling with emerald-colored glee. "We've missed you a lot. All of us have but how are you in this now moment dearest?"

"I'm wonderful! Just a moment ago, I was playing with my imagination on the swingset, flying like an eagle, and now I'm here! I'm so happy to be here again!" She paused to remember how throughout her life, she had been here many times before. She was so glad to have this memory back even if it would fade away again like Pachamama had said. A few creatures, including Felix the Fox, gathered below her and called out. They wanted to play too! Felix was so thrilled and couldn't wait to snuggle, so he jumped up into the tree. Lana hugged him closely and caressed his soft fur.

"Lana, I've missed you so much!"

"Hi, Felix! I've missed you too," she said. "It seems I'm beginning to forget this place. It makes me sad to admit that I can't remember the last time I saw you, but I do remember you, of course. I know that must be confusing. I'm sorry," she told him as she hugged him tighter.

"That's okay, Lana. We all knew that would happen. That's why we decided to make you something special, so you could remember us and have a part of us always with you," Felix said as he uncovered the most extraordinary necklace she'd ever seen. It was made from amber-coated, sage green shrubbery and ruby red flowers, strung together with orange carnelian and rose quartz stones. In the center was a glass jar filled with dust from the fairies' wings and something she had never seen before. It was mysterious and charmed yet also sturdy, able to withstand the tides of time.

The oak tree's branches gently gathered around Lana, supporting her affectionately. "The necklace will remind you of all that you need when the time is right. For now, enjoy this moment with your friends from the forest," Pachamama said.

Juniper and Marigold carefully took the necklace from Lana's hands and placed it around her neck. Lana was overcome with appreciation, barely able to contain all the love that she felt in her heart.

"I'll never take it off—it's incredible! Thank you," Lana said as tears of gratitude formed in the corner of her eyes. She hugged Felix and the fairies lovingly and continued to play in the tree. She felt like a mythical princess, adored and beloved by the forest. She was nourished by receiving such abundant love from nature.

Lana was a unique child, born into the world by young parents. Unfortunately, her father, Ray, left when Lana was almost two. She was raised by her mother, Rachel, and her grandmother, who she lovingly called Nana.

Most mornings, when Nana was at work, Lana and her young mother could be found at this small playground near their modest home. When the weather was pleasant, it was fitting for Rachel to work on the park bench and for Lana to express all of her magical energy with endless play. This was no ordinary playground of course, as it was next to the lush forest where Lana could connect with nature and be fully free.

She often wandered into the woods whenever she could slip away, and this day was no different. Rachel couldn't be bothered by searching for her daughter, and so impatiently she yelled: "Lana where are you? Get over here where I can see you! I'm trying to get this work done!"

Lana was startled and deeply wounded by the angry tone. Her eyes filled with tears as she scrambled down the tree and back towards the concrete playground. As she neared the edge of the forest, a black creature that she hadn't noticed scampered off. It growled softly, catching Lana by surprise. Stumbling, her crown crumbled, and all the creatures ran off. The enchantment quickly faded yet the necklace was intact. She felt startled by the dark animal and felt hurt from being yelled at. All she could do was weep.

"I'm sorry I yelled at you, baby. I just don't want you wandering off like that," her mother said remorsefully when Lana returned. She cradled and soothed Lana in her lap, uncovering chocolate from her bag.

"Where did you get that necklace, baby?"

"I got it from the forest," Lana said.

"It's stunning. Did Nana give it to you?"

"I got it from my other best friend," Lana said firmly.

Silence fell over the two of them. Rachel immediately returned to her work without seeing the magic right before her eyes. Lana was absorbed in the chocolate, but she still felt the forest singing out to her heart. Curious about the black creature, Lana wondered why it hadn't come up to the tree to play with her. Remembering his growl, she felt they must have both startled each other. Softly and tenderly, she hummed a song of deep gratitude back to each of the creatures in the forest.

She wished she could bring the essence of nature out into the world. She vowed to herself that she'd embody the ways of magic as best she could by using her imagination to bring the bliss of the forest out into the world around her. She placed her left hand on her necklace and set this intention with her whole heart.

As she did this, a large bird, flying high overhead, glided down past Lana and her mother, diving straight into the forest past the ancient oak tree of Pachamama. Soaring deeper into the woods, the majestic Condor was eager to share the events of Lana's visit with all of the forest. It was no small thing that the giving of the necklace had finally taken place. With every powerful flap of the Condor's wings, the forest lit up in ecstasy, glowing vibrantly at the news that a Child of Magic had received her magical birthright; a token of appreciation for her being. Inspired by the Condor's flight, the forest was living and breathing with ecstatic celebration. And like Lana, someone needed only to be open to notice it.

Wide Open Wings

Lana's quaint yellow house was a single story home. It had three small bedrooms, a tiny yard of mostly dirt and a lone sycamore tree in the back. Yet in Lana's imagination, the yard was an expansive desert, the tree a luscious oasis. She'd pretend she was on a quest, struggling to survive the harsh sandstorms and the heat. She would then reach what wasn't a mirage, but a sacred tree with its shade and fluttering leaves providing a haven for her to rest beneath.

Lana was an imaginative and curious child who loved books. Reading was another way to have an adventure. She liked climbing the backyard sycamore as high as she could to read her favorite stories. She appreciated the sycamore for the way it continually supported and inspired her.

Nana worked as a housekeeper for a wealthy family in a nearby neighborhood. It was easy for her to work hard and fast each day so she could get home to Lana, giving Rachel time to work or run errands.

One weekend, Rachel was making something special—

banana pancakes to break their weekly cereal routine. Drowsily, Lana was thinking of her dreams as she walked into the kitchen to have breakfast.

"Good morning, baby, how did you sleep? Did you have any dreams?" Rachel asked.

"I slept so well, Mama, and I even remembered how to fly last night."

"That's nice... Honey, are you ever going to take off that necklace?"

"No, I'm not. Please stop asking," Lana said plainly.

"Well okay, fine. So, you mean you dreamt you could fly?" Rachel asked with a slight edge to her voice.

"No, I dreamed that I could remember how to fly! I remembered that I had golden feathered wings that were larger than my body. They were connected to my shoulders and all I needed to do was want to fly and I could. My wings were glittering and when I flew, they shimmered like the rainbow. It was so beautiful." Lana sighed. "But when I woke up, they were gone. I'm sad that we forgot how to fly yet I know my wings will always be with me."

"Oh, baby, that's a lovely dream, but yours will leave

you as well. We all grow up eventually." Rachel said dismissively, as she flipped a pancake onto Lana's plate.

"We all have wings, and so do I, Mama! We just forget how to use them, just like we forget how to do a lot of things," Lana protested.

"I know, baby. Eat your pancakes, they're getting cold."

Lana didn't mention that after the dream, she'd awoken to find a winged angel in her doorway. Her eyes were sleepy from waking, but she clearly saw its glowing aura and felt its presence. With a blink, it vanished. Smiling, Lana thought about it while munching on her pancakes. She'd keep that moment to herself, because her mom probably wouldn't appreciate it anyway.

Rachel was the opposite of imaginative. Working as an accountant at a big chain clothing company, she was distant and distracted with her attention most often on her work. Her priority was to provide her small family with a life she was proud of. Being this way closed her off to the wonders that Lana was experiencing, which made it hard for them to feel a close bond.

Nana was a kind mother to Rachel, but her father wasn't

as caring. He had been a Marine in the Vietnam War, which made him a stern and harsh man. He hadn't shown Rachel much affection while she was growing up, but he had instilled in her a strong discipline that she carried with her. Even though he was a hardened man, Rachel wanted to make him proud, so she had always been an obedient child. That is until she met Lana's father, Ray, during their last year of high school. Ray was the new kid in school, and Rachel couldn't resist his free-spirited and charming demeanor. Rebelling against her father, they became high school sweethearts. Naturally, as they both loved each other, Lana was born into this world, a beautiful outcome of their adventurous and youthful love.

Rachel would often stare at her daughter, thinking how much like Ray she was. She wanted Lana to be more like herself and less like the wild, imaginative child she was already proving herself to be. Rachel was heartbroken by Ray's abandonment, so she determined that through hard work, she could instill a protective and focused nature in Lana.

Just before Lana's first year of school began, Rachel

decided to come home slightly earlier than usual to bake a special dessert, a family favorite, in hopes they could bond. There was only a couple of weeks before Lana would be starting school, and so Rachel wanted her to start off on the right path.

It was a cold night, and after eating Nana's savory soup for dinner, Rachel started to make her favorite zesty lemon-poppyseed cake. She wasn't the best chef, but she did her very best, especially with Lana's assistance. There was cake dust scattered about the kitchen as they had fun making a beautiful mess. Nana didn't wish to disturb the special time they were having, so she decided to go to bed earlier than usual so they could bake together.

"Mama, did Nana teach you how to bake?" Lana asked.

"No, not really," Rachel replied. "I was never really interested in cooking. The only reason I know this recipe is because your grandfather loved lemon cake."

"Oh, so Grandpa showed you how to make it?" Lana asked.

"Yes, he showed me when I was about your age, and so I always made it for him on his birthday. I've made it so many times, I can't seem to forget the recipe. Now it's become one of my favorites, too," Rachel laughed.

"Well then, I think it will be my favorite, too!" said Lana. They smiled at each other and put the cake in the oven.

While it was baking, Rachel began to make a cup of hot cocoa. Curiously, Lana asked, "Is this another treat Grandpa loved, Mama?"

"Well the cocoa is something we all enjoyed, just like you do now! But it was your father who had a special type of chocolate from his travels that he would make on special occasions. That kind isn't what we are used to. It is more bitter and not as sweet. Yet, just like the secret for the lemon cake is fresh lemons, the secret for the best chocolate is pure cacao!"

Lana was filled with such wonder as she imagined her ancestors making treats, cakes, and cups of chocolatey goodness, sharing them with so much love. She felt so comforted by hearing these memories of her father, and there was such a closeness with her mother that magical evening.

After finishing their cakes and cups of hot cocoa, Rachel decided to light the fireplace in the living room so they could be warm while they talked on the couch. They were usually in bed by now, but Rachel wanted to prepare Lana for her upcoming school year. Lana listened intently and enjoyed feeling the fire's warmth. She loved simply being with her mother even though they were talking about the most boring of topics.

While the fire burned gently, they sat together discussing the importance of school, getting good grades, and being focused until Lana went to bed.

Rachel decided to stay up a little longer to work. After dozing off on the couch, she woke groggily to the crackling fire. Blazing up to the ceiling, it engulfed the mantle, and dared to grow stronger still. She screamed over the flames, but no one could hear her! The hallway to the bedrooms was right next to the fireplace, so she couldn't get to the rooms from inside the house. She ran outside to Lana's bedroom and pounded on the glass window. Deep in sleep, Lana didn't move a muscle. By now, the smoke had gotten into the rooms! She put her sweater around her hand and smashed the window. With her primal motherly instincts kicking in, she tossed Lana onto her shoulders, carrying her out to the yard far from the house, and then ran back inside to find her mother.

Lana woke up to see the flames escaping through the living room window and out into the moonlight. They were dancing in the most disturbing way that made her feel dizzy and sick to her stomach. The fire seemed to be crying out for her attention. It was a haunting sight! Lana was frightened until she saw her mother and Nana escaping the house as they came over to where she was waiting. Once Lana knew they were all going to be okay, she could catch her breath. Settling into herself, she felt that her wings must have guided her safely out of the fire. Feeling her magic return, Lana could see an essence in the flames and smoke. The Fire sang out to her:

"Pause. Presence. Peace.

Thoughts of fear may come, but pause and be still, finding love and peace wherever you go.

We can choose loving thoughts over and over again.

Every moment of every day is a chance to start again, like the Phoenix rising from the ashes, we can rise in love."

Lana felt peace and courage course through her whole

body. She looked down to see her necklace glowing and then looking back behind her, she could see her own wings! They were the same as those of the angel she had seen in the doorway, and she felt her whole body tingle. Envisioning her wings fanning out to cover her family in a loving embrace, she felt assured that she could keep Nana and her mother safe.

"Hear this: A child that feels responsible for the ones they love, will learn throughout life that no one is responsible for another.

It begins and ends within you.

Child, you will learn,

You are appreciated and loved for your courage, but you must love yourself first.

To love and be loved, that is your purpose.

Release into my transforming fires the need to save and shelter others, and instead, simply fly and be who you are."

The Fire finished singing its song, and just like Pachamama's, it was conveyed through a language of deep loving. Lana released her tight grip of the necklace and let the vision of her wings fade, falling asleep in her mother's arms.

When the fire department arrived, they stopped the fire from spreading through the whole house. The living room was destroyed, but everything else was spared. It took weeks to get the house repaired, and much longer to get the haunted memory of that fearful night out of Rachel's and Nana's heads. But instead of being afraid, Lana stayed in her magic and remembered what the Fire had sung. This planted a seed for Lana, and now she knew how to find her purpose, presence, and peace.

Lana felt like nature, even when intense like the house fire, was benevolent and truly nurturing if loved and cared for in return. She only wished to fully express her magic, showing others how to be close with nature and shine wonderfully, even in the midst of fear. Lana knew that by being open to her magic, Pachamama would be fully devoted to helping her fulfill her purpose. Feeling that people were not as open to magic as she was, Lana wished her wings could expand far enough so she could be an example for all to see. Guided by her necklace, she knew her magic would always show her the way.

Lessons from the Sea

As Lana grew older, just as Pachamama had told her, the connection to her magic slowly began to fade. But up until then, she had used her necklace as a constant reminder. Her sparkling imagination had made it easy to stay connected to the magic and close to her truth. Lana was a wondrous beam of light to behold in a dimming world that was slowly being overtaken by the Shadows.

One of her favorite places to shine was near the ocean! On warm Sundays, Rachel, Nana, and Lana went to the beach. By the sea, Lana could easily explore her magic and be left alone with her creations for hours on end. Lana noticed the waves calmed her mother and Nana sat peacefully, always encouraging Lana to play freely.

On this particularly magical Sunday, while Nana and Rachel prepared lunch, Lana was peacefully playing on the seashore. She was on a quest to pick out blue and green stones from the sand, collecting them for her friends from the forest. With every new wave that washed over her feet,

Lana began to notice that she couldn't feel the difference between her skin and the water. As she closed her eyes, her feelings stretched out in front of her as far as her mind's eye could see. She began to soften and surrender by fully feeling the ocean. Sensing this, the Sea sang out to her:

"Come to me, sweet child, return to the sea.

Soothingly reminding you how simple it is to be,

may you remember,

your truest nature is within these vast waters.

You are destined for great softness and infinite strength."

Remembering the songs from the Fire and Pachamama, Lana felt another part of her heart opening up from the song of the Sea. The elements were opening her more fully to her truth; the water washing away all forgetfulness of her wholeness.

Lana was ecstatic, flowing up from the water and dancing to the rhythm of the waves. When she listened carefully, nature always had a recognizable tune. As she moved, her necklace continued to lay perfectly on her heart. She had fully surrendered to the ocean's song, beaming like a rainbow of colors that spread out in all directions.

Immersed in this moment of bliss, Lana began to sense that everything was not all light, that there was something amiss. She noticed a shadow swirling all around her. It was coming from the depths of the ocean, lifting up from the land, and sinking down from the sky. Startled, she opened her eyes, and it immediately vanished! Something within her remembered this feeling, and while it did seem scary, she sensed that the darkness was just as curious as she was.

Soon she began to grow weary from so much movement. She sat down on the sand to look out over the Sea. In the waters she saw a familiar face look up at her! Pachamama's spirit was in the ocean, swimming peacefully.

"Hello, Pachamama! Are you the Sea as well?" Lana asked with some confusion.

"Dear one, I am the Earth you now rest on, the Air you breathe, the Sea you feel, and the Fire that came to you in the night. I move through these elements to awaken the magic of the world. And just like you, my dear, I am here for all that will remember me. Take the messages of the Sea, the teachings of the Fire, remain grounded on the Earth, and do your very best to remember that you breathe in my spirit with every single breath you take."

Lana held her hand to her heart, feeling her chest breathing and moving to the motion of the ocean. Not sensing any more shadows, she once again felt completely at home and safer than ever before.

Opening her eyes, she looked out and saw a mermaid swimming towards her. "Hi!" Lana squealed with excitement. She remembered it was always the highlight of her beach trips to see the princess of the Sea with her striking pale blue eyes, silver skin, and regal purple hair.

"It is so wonderful to see you again, sweet kindred spirit. Here is the treasure I promised to show you last time," said the mermaid, handing Lana a beautiful shell. "It's a gift from the sea, just for you."

Lana put it close to her heart and then held it up to the sky. Gold and pink hues shimmered in the sun, blinding her momentarily. She quickly looked back towards the gorgeous mermaid.

"This is amazing. I love it. Thank you so much!" She hadn't recalled that the mermaid would be giving her a gift, and she was too shocked to admit it. However, she did remember reading that mermaid appearances were extremely rare, and so she tried not to blink, as the mermaid might disappear under the water at any second. "You're quite welcome," the mermaid called out to Lana "It's from the same source of love as your necklace, and it is very precious. Remember to treat it with love and care. Just like how you can love and treasure yourself, sweet child. Will you remember that?"

"Yes. I will always!" Lana said, thinking to herself that she could never forget.

Sensing Lana's determination, the mermaid felt she had done all she could to help her remember. "Wonderful! It was my mission to give you this, and so now I must be going. I have more magical business to attend to—for you know who," the mermaid motioned behind her, where Pachamama's face could still be seen stirring up the waters. "I will see you next time, Lana."

"Okay, goodbye!" Lana yelled past the growing strength of the crashing surf. She waved as she watched the mermaid disappear beneath the sea. Full of joy, she pranced over to show her mother and Nana the treasured gift.

"Look, Nana and Mama! This is a gift from my mermaid

friend," Lana bubbled.

"That's lovely," Rachel said sarcastically. "Are you hungry?" she asked, holding out a sandwich.

Sensing the indifference, Nana reassured Lana: "That's so beautiful, sweetie. We will make sure to keep it safe when we get home, so you can have it forever. And I have just the thing for you to place all your treasures in!"

Lana smiled at her Nana and then turned to stare at her mother. She shook her head no to the sandwich and said nothing.

It wasn't a surprise that her mother didn't understand her, but it was still so disappointing. Her mother didn't seem to see things the same as Lana did. It was as if her mother was covered in a veil of gray fog that hid the vibrancy of life from her. Lana saw things with vivid clarity, and Nana continually encouraged this way of living.

Lana was appreciative of Nana's magic, yet wished her own mother could see clearly, too. Since she had no words, she got up to display her magic. She flowed and danced around with her golden wings. This was her way of encouraging her mother and all those around her to be magical and express themselves, too. Lana was a mirror for those she loved, even though they were distracted by their own lives. She reflected to them who they truly were: Children of Magic.

Rachel didn't see it, and this time, even Nana missed it as well. Yet Pachamama was glowing all around, glistening through each of the elements, appreciating the harmonious way Lana interacted with magic and nature. Sending the breeze to gently caress Lana's face, and lifting up the sand to shimmer all around her, Pachamama helped her feel how loved she really was. Her magic was still strong, even though she was the only one open to seeing it.

Sharing The Magic

It was the weekend of Lana's birthday party, and she only had one friend to invite. Well, one human friend that is. She also invited her best friends from the forest to join in the festivities. She even asked the creatures from the sea, not completely sure how they'd arrive. For her birthday, Rachel got her some books that had pages to color in. To Lana's dismay, Rachel spent most of the day running in and out of the house, busy with weekend errands. Nana gifted her a beautiful china set for drinking hot cocoa, and as she had promised, she gave her a jasper wooden box to keep all her treasures in.

Together they set out the new china with Nana's baked goods, Rachel's lemon-poppyseed cake, and hot cocoa. The yard smelled like a scrumptious bakery as the scent of their delicious desserts filled the yard. Nana placed the candles into the cake in the shape of a heart. Carefully, she lit them and told Lana to wish for anything her heart desired. Lana placed her hand over her necklace and sweetly asked for the most magical birthday she could ever hope to have.

Hearing her call carried across the breeze, the wind swept through the yard, carrying with it Juniper, Marigold, and Felix! Wind and leaves swirled around her, sending her into pure delight. The trees began to sway and dance, sending more leaves spiraling up into the sky. The fires on the candles burned more brightly, and the water in their cups lifted. It was as if time slowed down and gravity became suspended within the magic. Lana watched as her friends danced around her yard, noticing Nana standing with her mouth wide open.

Both were still unable to speak as the table transformed into a breathtaking feast of treats. Stretching across the entire yard, it was fully covered in cakes, pies, biscuits with fresh jams, and sweet creams with berries on top. There were cupcakes, caramels, cookies, and a chocolate fountain, too!

"Hi Lana!" bubbled Felix. "Thank you for calling in the elements so we could join you! Here, we made matching party hats from the forest. Now let's all wear them and have a grand time. You only turn six years old once, you know!" In one swift movement, he grabbed a chocolate cupcake from the table, eating it in one bite before he even sat down. Juniper and Marigold giggled with elation.

"The hats go perfectly with my necklace and birthday outfit. Thank you!" Lana said. They all sat down, gave thanks, and enjoyed their many desserts. "Your Nana is such a superb baker, and this hot cocoa is quite magical," Felix said. "Please do give my compliments to the chef."

"Simply marvelous," agreed Marigold.

"Well, some of these are from my mother and my Nana," Lana explained. "Like the lemon cake and the special drinks. I am so happy to share all these magical treats with my best friends!" Lana was overflowing with boundless joy.

Sensing a special magic in the air, the mermaid appeared, taking Lana by surprise.

"Why hello again, your majesty," Lana curtsied. "I am so happy you found a way to come and join us today!"

Lana was happy to have the majestic mermaid and the spirit of the Sea present at her party in their small kiddie pool. The mermaid sat in the sunshine next to where Pachamama's presence manifested in the trunk of the sycamore tree.

Lana's school friend Megan wasn't able to join the

celebration until it was very close to ending, and by that time, all of her magical friends had left. They had already enjoyed the entire morning together filled with treats, dancing, and play.

Soon after Megan arrived, Rachel surprised the girls with freshly made pizza. They joined together and ended the celebration with a dinner party. Sufficiently satisfied from so many treats, Lana and Megan laid on the grass to watch the sky turn into cotton candy colors. Lana would stick her tongue out to taste the clouds and delighted in which flavors she preferred. Megan would observe and smile but not once did she take part in trying to use her imagination. They stayed out in the yard watching the clouds until it became dusk and the stars lit up the darkening sky.

"How did you like your birthday?" Megan asked.

"It was all perfect," Lana replied. "One of my favorite parts of the day was when the mermaid accidentally splashed water on Marigold and she fell into the pool, turning the water into a lovely shade of opal. Since she got wet, Marigold decided to swim for the rest of the morning and the water remained so beautiful."

Lana had mentioned her forest and ocean friends to Megan before, but it never seemed to phase Megan.

"I don't know if you really are made of magic or if you're just pretending? I always seem to miss seeing your friends with my real eyes," said Megan.

"Yes, well, Pachamama says, *"One needs only to be open to notice it."* If you aren't willing to sense the magic around you, then it's easy to miss," Lana said.

"Well at my house it isn't allowed, and my parents told me that make-believe things aren't real," Megan said. "Yet, I like listening to your stories."

Lana thought about uncovering her golden wings so that Megan could see that magic does exist, yet she decided it wasn't the time. When the right moment presented itself, she'd show the world. Nana called them into the house because it was getting dark outside, and so they raced inside.

A week after her birthday party, Lana was over at Megan's. Megan was a sweet child, and her parents let them play outside in the mysterious backyard. They played for hours, without being interrupted.

While many would have seen the land as a bit of a

junkyard, to the girls, it was an estate. The main house was at the front of the property, and there was even another house in the back. On the left side of this large plot of land were abandoned motorhomes, piles of scrap metal, and large stacks of wood; all homes for the most mysterious critters and creatures! The girls spent most of their time playing right in the middle of the property. Here, they had a sanctuary below a grove of trees where they'd sit in the grassy dirt making mud pies, drawing, collaging, and making other creations. Lana invited her fairy friends to join in on the fun making the concoctions. Megan couldn't see the magic yet she could sense something was different about Lana when she was using her imagination. Lana and Megan loved to play hide and seek among the junk, dance in the sun, and do cartwheels until they got dizzy. The fairies helped show Lana how to flip and tumble like the fairy gymnast she really was. Megan was having fun yet could sense Lana was especially enjoying her time.

Aware of Megan's curiosity, Lana sat down to rest. Wanting to shine her light and magic to her friend, she told this story:

"Once upon a time, in a faraway land, there was a plain village with no color. In the center of the village was a large hill, and at the top lay a saffron cactus flower, shimmering amidst the colorless environment. Hidden from plain sight, it patiently waited to be discovered. Each day, it blossomed with bright hues, yet no one could see or appreciate it. For many years, it bloomed each and every day, trying its best to be found. One day, a young child was born without sight or hearing, yet he bore wings! Once he was old enough to use his unique gifts, he flew up to the hill and touched the flower with loving adoration. The flower, patiently waiting to be remembered, thanked the boy for feeling him and released a mist from its petals that washed over the entire land. Once the magical mist lifted, it revealed a vibrancy of all colors that finally returned to the village."

Megan was entranced and so Lana continued.

"The villagers wanted to know how the blind boy knew there was a curse on the land and that an enchanted flower needed to be found to release it. They also asked why the flower did not help him with his own shortcomings. The boy glided up to the sky to convey an answer, yet he could not communicate like they did. The villagers saw his flight but some grew irritated as they didn't understand his way of communicating, and so they dismissed him. In their denial, some remained cursed. If they had tried to understand him, they would have seen that he was special in his own way and didn't need to change for the world around him. He was perfect as he was."

Lana continued, "If they had only looked up from their drab village up into the sky, they would have recognized that there are even more colors than the rainbow reveals. They needed only to gaze long enough and feel into it, stripping away the old way of seeing. As the boy flew higher and further away, he never returned to the place where no one understood him. Instead, he traveled to a land full of his own kind; a place where people's gifts and differences were celebrated and treasured. Every year since the magical boy lifted the curse, some of the villagers gather to sing loud songs of gratitude and to remember his magic. They threw powdered colors into bonfire flames so all shades of the rainbow could be seen in the billowing smoke. They remembered the boy with the magical vision and wings to fly, and have seen their own village in that light ever since. The end," said Lana.

"Wow, Lana. How do you come up with this stuff? It's so interesting and sometimes strange. But I like it!" said Megan.

"Sometimes I see it and sometimes I dream about it," said Lana.

"What does it all mean? Why were the villagers still cursed?" asked Megan.

"The boy was magic. A guide. But many villagers weren't listening or truly looking to see. He couldn't stay there if no one was going to listen, and so by his actions, he was an example for them all," Lana said.

"Wow, I get it! Sort of... I mean, I think I get it," said Megan.

"It's okay if you don't yet. Just let it sink into your heart and try to remember to be like the ones who believed," Lana said with hope in her own heart. They sat there silently remembering for a while.

Then Lana spoke up: "I have an idea. I'm going to call forth the fairy sisters—if you'd like to play with us?

They live very close by, and I am sure you'd all get along wonderfully! Would you like to give it a chance?"

"I don't know! I'm scared." said Megan.

"You have no reason to be."

"What if my Parents find out?"

"They won't." Lana smiled reassuringly.

"Alright. I'll try."

Okay, sit there and close your eyes. Let's see." Lana placed her hands on her necklace and over her heart. Closing her eyes, she envisioned flying into the forest to gather Marigold and Juniper on her back, bringing them to where she and Megan were. In her mind's eye, she saw them at the oak where they lived; they looked back at her with joy. Lana smiled and opened her eyes to see them there in front of her now.

"You've come! I'm so excited to introduce you to my friend Megan!" Lana said.

"Hello child, it is so wonderful to meet a friend of Lana's!" said Marigold, and both fairies curtseyed in midair, twinkling as they moved.

Megan just stared in awe. Lana giggled.

"We want to also introduce you girls to a friend of ours as well. She actually lives here in Megan's magical estate. She's timid, yet she has tried to get your attention from time to time, Megan. I think now is the perfect time to be formally introduced," said Juniper. "Butter! Come out so we can all see you."

"Oh, my goodness. They really do exist. I'm so sorry I ever doubted you, Lana. This is amazing!" exclaimed Megan.

A beautiful bumble bee came their way and spoke sweetly. "Hello there, sisters. Hello, Lana, and hello, neighbor. I'm Butter the Bee," she said. As she flew closer, Megan could see how cute Butter's tiny expressions were and how cuddly her fuzzy body seemed. This was her first time looking closely at a bee, and she wondered why she had been so afraid before. "It's wonderful to finally make your acquaintance," said Butter.

"Pleased to make your acquaintance as well," Megan replied. "I have seen you before, but I always ran away from you because my mother warned me about being stung. I'm so sorry! That must have hurt your feelings."

"Thank you for your apology. I was sad, but I understood why you might be frightened. Some bees get a bad rap, but we are mostly a friendly species," said Butter.

"Well I am so grateful to have a neighbor like you. I thought Lana was probably the only one to have special friends near her, but I'd love to be your friend and play together," said Megan.

Butter the Bee landed on Megan's fingertip which made her giggle and so she petted the fuzzy creature softly. They all played together for hours until it got dark. Lana was so pleased. She could feel that her magic was spreading into the world around her and it felt so right.

The girls and the creatures enjoyed a couple of summers in this way, until things began to change. As summer turned into autumn, the time when the leaves change colors, Lana saw the rainbow of magic spreading through the forest. She walked through the back gate of the magical estate to get to their special grove of trees. When she arrived, she found mud pies and pretend coffees sitting out on the table! However, something was unusual. Megan, Butter, Juniper, and Marigold all sat there solemnly waiting for her arrival.

She instantly knew something was going on.

"Hi everyone. I'm so happy to see all of you here, and all of this lovely food, but please, tell me what's wrong? I know something's up," said Lana.

"Well," said Megan, "I hoped we could play first before I gave you the bad news, but it's impossible to pretend like nothing is the matter." The others bowed their heads and closed their eyes, knowing the news would sadden Lana. "I'm moving, Lana. My father got a new job, and he's making us all leave. It just isn't fair! I'm so sad Lana. I will miss you and the magic forever."

"I will miss you, yet the magic is inside you Meg," said Lana.

" I think you can see it for me but I can't see it for myself. I've never seen magic when I was alone and I can already feel it starting to fade," said Megan.

Everything she was feeling was indescribable, and so she said nothing more. Her heart ached terribly as she held her friend while they both cried. After feeling so much sadness, they remembered they still had a full day of play ahead of them! They decided to spend their last day together fully immersed in magic and play. The wind blew its colorful leaves into the backyard so the girls and the fairies could jump into piles of earth and feel held by Pachamama. The backyard on their last day looked more magical than ever, covered with colorful leaves and sprinkled with fairy dust.

Lana was eight years old when Megan left. She had lost her best friend and was afraid she would never have a friend like that again.

The other children at school thought Lana was different and weird. She never took off her enchanted necklace and was bullied because of it. Only occasionally did some of the children at school talk to her, and she only got invited to a party one time.

The week before Halloween, Sandy, one of the popular girls at school, gathered with her friends in the courtyard to invite Lana. It was Sandy's Halloween party and the girls made sure to tell her it was a dress up party.

"Hey Lana, why don't you ever take off that funny necklace of yours?" asked Sandy.

"Because it was a special gift, and I cherish it dearly," retorted Lana.

The girls snickered and Sandy held back from jeering. "Okay, whatever you say. Well I wanted to invite you to my party. We're all going to dress up as our favorite animals, and I thought I'd be nice enough to invite you, too, since your friend Megan just moved and all. But I'm not sure if you could dress up if you won't ever take your necklace off?" said Sandy, making all the girls laugh. There was a moment of silence as the girls waited for a reaction from Lana.

"Well, I'll see if I can make it. Thanks for letting me know." Lana said, trying to remain grounded as a feeling of nervousness came over her.

The day of the party, Lana decided she'd go and give Sandy and her friends a chance. She decided to dress up as Felix the Fox. She loved dressing up and equally loved him, so she really enjoyed preparing for the occasion. She hid her necklace underneath the costume so no one could see it. Her cute little tail was sewn onto the back of a red-and-white jumper with sweet fluffy ears and a black nose painted on perfectly by Nana. Lana was having so much fun, that is until she arrived at the party and realized that it wasn't a Halloween party at all. It was actually a birthday party and she was the only one dressed up. Sandy and the girls surrounded her, laughing at her costume.

Lana didn't resist that she was unique, yet she could feel herself brimming with anger. She couldn't remember who had told her, but someone once told her she was perfect as she was. She liked the fact that she was dressed up, but being deceived hurt her heart. She went into the bathroom, and looking into the mirror, she called out to Felix.

"Whoa, okay! Nice costume Lana," said Felix as he jumped up on the sink. "I heard what the girls said to you. You have good reason to be angry."

Flustered, Lana opened up to her best friend. "It just hurts my heart that I'm the only one who likes to be magical and people just can't see it. And then they try to make me feel like the crazy one!"

"I know how much you like to play like the fairy sisters yet for today, how about you shine your magic a different way?"

Lana liked that idea, so she smeared the black paint from her nose around her eyes creating a dark, mysterious look.

43

Baring her teeth and smiling at herself, she liked feeling her wild side. She calmly strolled out of the bathroom as steam rolled out eerily behind her. Feeling mischievous, she danced around the girls as they looked on with astonishment. With a flick of her tail, she tipped over a vase, shattering it on the ground.

"Oops. I must not be used to my tail."

"You better fix that vase or my mom is going to ruin me. Why don't you use your magic and put it back together!" Sandy was scared by Lana's fearless expression, trying to once again make her look silly.

"Magic comes from the heart, something you don't know about yet." Lana jumped towards Sandy with a growl. Instead of being playful and acting like a little creature with Lana, Sandy dismissed her with a flick of her hand and went to find a broom.

She never bonded with another school friend like Megan, and so she preferred to stay on her own and play in her own way. Months went by, and Lana recognized that she felt safe within herself and found great comfort reading books. Opening a book made her feel welcomed, and she found herself in the pages of fantastic stories of all sorts. Her imagination could be safely contained within books unlike in the distorted world of disillusionment. However, while she felt fully safe retreating into her own world, what she didn't yet know is that little seeds of hardness had begun to sprout in her heart. She did not know any better. She was doing what all people tend to do when experiencing pain. She did what she needed at that time, to feel safe and at home in her own body.

The Fog of Disenchantment

Lana believed in magic for far longer than the average child. With her powerful imagination, she was able to resist the disenchantment that comes with aging and worldly rules. She was perceived as different yet she was very pretty and smart. Others always judged her by her outward qualities, and so within, her true-self began to drift astray, unable to resist the ways of the world around her. She began to slip into complete forgetfulness. Feeling different, she began to feel lonely and isolated.

One day, when Lana was about ten years old, she was with her mother at the neighborhood grocery store. The market always made her feel uneasy with its harsh, artificial lighting and hurried people. The shoppers seemed like zombies, which made Lana uncomfortable. She had been so busy with her studies and lost in her books, that being in the outside world made her feel detached to herself and to those around her.

Lana was in the only aisle she liked, the cereal aisle,

when she saw a new vibrant red and green cereal box that reminded her of a shimmering memory. She remembered how she used to love dancing with fairies, and at that moment, she wished to see her magical friends. With that desire in her heart, she took a deep breath, placed a hand over her muted necklace, and summoned them with her mind's eye. Just for a moment, she imagined that the beautiful glowing fairy sisters of the forest came to comfort her and play in the aisles. Suddenly, Juniper and Marigold flew out from behind the cereal boxes and eagerly showed themselves! They glowed with a heavenly aura, glimmering with golden hues that lit up the aisle with their magic. They invited her to dance and play, forgetting the cold store and its sleepy people.

Lana remembered she held the power to bring her magic back with her imagination! She followed the fairies in movement while they flew and chirped happily, twirling and dancing together in a loving reunion. Lana giggled at the fairy dust that tickled her nose. With gratitude in her heart, she took a deep breath, and once again she beamed with her own golden, radiant aura.

"I know it's been a very long time, and I've been so busy with homework and chores, but I've missed you! Thank you for being here." She was so thankful and could barely believe this was happening.

"We've missed dancing and playing with you Lana, we're always here whenever you need us," whispered Juniper. She flew up close to Lana and gave her a quick kiss on the cheek. Marigold blew a crimson-dusted kiss that landed on Lana's other cheek.

"I love playing with you, it's just sometimes I forget you're around," said Lana.

Felix the fox dashed from around the corner of the aisle, and jumped up, toppling Lana to the floor with affection. "It's so wonderful to see you! And you're wearing your beautiful necklace! You've grown so much since the last time we saw you."

"You look mischievous as always, Felix." Lana laughed and got up from the ground. "And the sisters look stunning as ever. I've missed you all tremendously."

Lana sadly remembered that she was told not to use her imagination and play with her magical friends when they were out in public. Her mother said that it was okay to use her imagination in private, only if it didn't interfere with her responsibilities. She also said that it was inappropriate at this age and it might disturb her "normal development." Although she knew her mother was trying to do her best, Lana felt misunderstood and isolated, discouraged from being herself.

Besides Rachel's rebellious yet magical relationship with Ray, she was always serious just like her own father. She felt obligated to be disciplined and so she let the process of growing up constrict her play and dampen her magic. When Ray left her, she was determined to work hard and raise Lana strictly. Being productive and staying busy was fine by her. She loved crunching numbers, and graduated from college with a degree in finance. Accounting would be her chosen love affair, and she made it clear a "real love life" didn't matter anymore. Relationships hadn't served her well, and now she had her daughter to care for. She suppressed her feelings by placing her attention on things outside herself.

Caught in her own reality, Rachel interrupted her daughter's fun in the cereal aisle. "What are you still doing over here? Stay close to me. I need you to handle the cart while I check off this list." Lana sighed and sadly gestured for her friends to scatter; they vanished. Lana's heart hurt, but she remained loyal to her mother and with an aching heart, walked over to grab the cart. Just like that, her imagination crumbled, her light dimmed, and her true essence faded.

Lana was helping her mother put the groceries away in the trunk of the car when the wind began picking up, blowing leaves through the parking lot. She paused to look up at the leaves that lifted into the sky, reminding her of her own wings that she'd so often forgotten. She stood there trying to remember what they looked like as she watched the Wind flow all around.

As she stood in the parking lot, she felt so small looking up at the vast sky. She could faintly see Pachamama's face in the wind as she was dancing within the flowing leaves. The winds shifted, picking up colorful wildflowers, carrying a fanciful melody sung high in the sky. Its song rose and fell, coming down to flow in and around people in the parking lot, yet only Lana saw its majesty.

"Grown-ups are always in a hurry. Keeping themselves

busy so they never have to feel deeply about why they are so discontented from being disconnected with me, their Mother. If they paused and grounded into the Earth, they would hear me lovingly whisper in their ear," howled the Wind.

Pachamama willed the wispy winds into a powerful, thunderous lightning storm. "As you grow, you tend to lose your ability to hear me clearly, but I am always here. I never leave, not even when you're lost in your thoughts or actions." The wind swept down, glittering with illumination around a baby carriage in the parking lot. The child cooed, smiling up at the dark, impending sky, laughing as the first drizzle of rain splashed on his small toes. Slowly, fog from the dew rolled in as it poured rain. Rachel thought aloud to herself, "My hair is going to get so frizzy with this crazy weather," as she threw the rest of the groceries into the trunk of the car and slammed it shut.

Lana's mood mirrored the dark weather that swept overhead. Feeling depressed and trapped in the backseat of the car, she could feel the Shadows taking her over. She pressed her forehead to the window and closed her eyes. She was lost in thought and missed hearing Pachamama in the whispering winds. Too tired to care, she looked up slowly as the rain poured down the window, covering her view.

Shadows Creep In

The week right before winter break arrived in a blink. Most kids had made Christmas lists, but Lana hadn't started on hers. She was busy with school projects and had not even read any of her favorite Christmas stories. Lana was working diligently when music and delicious scents reminded her of the joyful season. Feeling a breath of inspiration, she set down her work and gave her imagination a chance, coming up with a toy story. Her favorite holiday fairytale story was visiting the crystal lake and its friendly creatures on the way to the North Pole. She loved creating fantastical holiday stories but hadn't done so since the year before, back when she used to give her imagination much more exercise.

She picked up her dolls with enthusiasm, only to quickly realize that her imagination was too muddled to play with her magic.

"Okay guys, I know it's been a while but where were we?" Lana said doubtfully. "Prancer, you were saying something about the dazzling dolphins, am I right?" She squinted with impatience and didn't get a reply.

With a heavy heart, she sighed and put the toys down. Lana had forgotten how to create from her truth, just as Pachamama foretold. As she put the toys away, her heart ached but she thought to herself, *it's time to grow up.*

For now this was true. Lana was growing up quickly and she had many responsibilities given to her by her mother to keep her busy. From this agreement, Lana became an overachiever. Not wanting to give her mother any worries, she strove to get straight As in school. Rachel approved of Lana's discipline, but Nana was quietly unsupportive of this strict arrangement. On many occasions, she tried to get Lana to remember her creativity but to no avail. The pull to get her mother's approval was incontestable.

Lana sat on her bean-bag and put a thoughtless show on the TV and let herself be swept away with a story that numbed and muted her senses. Her aura dimmed, and her necklace faded.

Nana knocked on the door and walked in slowly with a plate of cookies. "Hi, Lana, I was wondering if you'd like to play with me while we munch on some chocolate chip cookies? I'm trying out a new recipe for Santa, so let me know if it's a good one. And maybe you'd like to start creating a Christmas list tonight?" Nana asked tentatively.

"You can leave some cookies, but I can't play right now, Nana. I'm too tired. Besides, Santa isn't real; that's what everyone at school says. Also, I have a big test in my first period class tomorrow." She paused and then sadly confessed, "And I know the Tooth Fairy isn't real because I left my tooth with a little piece of chocolate in a note. I put it next to the lantern and no fairy came to get it this last time. When I told Mom, she said she totally forgot about the tooth. So now I know that it was all you and Mom pretending to be Santa, the Tooth Fairy, and the Easter Bunny, too. So, I don't need a list. I just want to get a dress and a new pair of shoes, but I can tell Mom myself." Lana was holding her breath as she blurted out her thoughts, gasping for air when she finished speaking. Hiding tears, Lana snapped her head back to face the TV and away from her Nana.

"Oh, okay." Nana walked towards Lana with cookies in hand and sat next to her. "You're right, sweetie. Those things aren't exactly real, they're just fun for your imagination.

But I hope you don't forget that there is still magic within and all around you. It is a different type of magic that is available to you anytime through your heart." Nana said no more, kissing Lana on the forehead, sighing deeply as she left the room.

Nana was such a sweet and kind soul. She always brought a warm presence without effort, living lovingly and tenderly. Close to her loved ones, she was ready and willing to please others because it made her joyful to see those around her happy. She could sense that Lana was transitioning like all children do as they grow up in the modern world, when the density of that world seeps in and weighs heavy on the heart. It was difficult to see Lana's sense of wonder and light fade, but Nana also trusted in the divinity of how all things happened, so she didn't spend much time dwelling on it. She was easy-going and loving with her beliefs. She spent her Sunday mornings at the church down the street, praying each day that things in her and her family's lives happened with ease and grace. This was her own way in which she stayed connected to her magic; walking lightly upon the Earth and being a safe place for her loved ones.

Outside a rush of wind was raging to be heard. Lana didn't move or look away from the TV, and so she didn't notice the chaos outside. Pachamama and the Shadow were facing off in an intense storm of energy. The Shadow was overtaking the window, coming into the room, covering Lana in darkness. The light bounced off the window and danced with gleaming colorful leaves that led all the way up to the twilight sky.

Even amidst the Shadow, Pachamama's golden aura was radiating through the window. Peacefully she sang:

"I will always remain in your heart sweet child, patiently waiting for you to hear my whispers, to feel your truth again. I am forever near.

I sing with the mesmeric melody that wills shivers.

I collide with the crashing waves.

I set with the vibrant sun.

I stir up rustling leaves to connect with the sky.

I am in all things.

I am naturally loving, nurturing, and enduring.

I knowingly wait for the moment you feel me, come back to me, or become one with me again."

Pachamama's glistening outline remained by the window for a moment, but her winds and leaves swept back into the forest. The enchantment faded away as the fog of worldly illusion covered the magic with its dark shadows.

Lana found growing up to be confusing and quite hard at times, yet she met her experiences head-on with fierce determination. This difficulty was made even more challenging because the further away she got from shining her light, the more the shadows of life blocked her truth. She could remember seeing the Shadow many times throughout her young life, like when she was dancing with the ocean or seeing it in the storm clouds at the supermarket. However, she never quite knew what to make of it. The more her light dimmed, the closer the Shadow crept in, hardening her heart.

One Saturday morning when Lana was thirteen years old, she was in her backyard sitting on one of the lower branches of the sycamore reading a book. She still liked being outdoors but now there was distance between her and nature. Even though Lana was no longer listening, Pachamama remained present, whispering while Lana read.

"Life can sometimes be soft, and sometimes be hard. Life

is filled with traumas large and small, full of deep darkness and magnificent light. Without experiencing these lessons, there can be no understanding or compassion, sweet child."

Pachamama sang this compassionately as she supported Lana through the essence of the sycamore, preparing her for all that was yet to come. Lana would eventually discover that her experiences were exactly what was needed for her to grow and evolve. In divine timing, she'd be able to transmute the vast love from within her heart to everyone and everything around her. Only with a blossomed heart could she transform her lessons into compassion and return to her magic. At the moment, however, she was foraging her own way, out of alignment with nature and forgetting her truth.

Books kept Lana's attention, and she also spent more time watching TV. Sometimes she'd read sweet, fanciful books, but gradually, they became darker as the Shadow completely surrounded her life. She was in a phase where she liked hearing about ghost stories and haunted houses. Spooky books thrilled her and also shadowed her own pain and fear. She masked her own feelings by being consumed by the fright of someone else's story. She played less and became distracted more. She'd be enamored by other people's stories for hours. Rachel didn't care what books were read, as long as they were considered age-appropriate—and only after homework was completed.

Lana was reading about a possessed puppet that was controlled by a floating black cape when her mother came over and gently tapped her on her foot. "Lana, how would you feel if I told you your father was back and that he wants to speak to you?" Rachel asked tenderly.

"Ummm, what? I would think you were joking, but I think it would be amazing," she responded quickly and felt a bit dizzy.

"Okay, sweetie. Well, I have a big surprise for you, and I'm not joking. Your father is in town. He found out where we live through your uncle, and he's at your favorite café right this minute. I know this could be overwhelming, but would you like to go see him right now?"

Lana shrieked, "Yes, of course!" Her face flushed and her heart beat rapidly. She was unable to express the magnitude of what she felt with words or emotions, but her eyes widened and her smile became unsteady. She was confused, excited, happy, sad, and more than anything, startled. She had always wanted to say the strange word "Dad" out loud to her father like other children got to. She had dreamt of having a father figure to discuss the things that she couldn't with her mother. She had always felt something missing in her life without really recognizing it was him, until just now.

She imagined them talking about the stars and all the galaxies in the universe. She wanted to show him places like her favorite forest and trees, now a distant memory from her childhood. The image of them sharing hot cocoa and lemon-poppyseed cake flashed in her mind, and she knew she'd never tell anyone that she had fantasized about this many times before. She had butterflies in her tummy, and she felt a rush of warmth flow through her. She was nervous. She jumped from the tree and landed gracefully on her feet with the assistance of her wings. Beaming with excitement, she stepped forward with an open heart, ready to finally greet her father.

Mother and daughter walked into the café side by side. It smelled of coffee and burnt toast. It was a bit too bright, making Lana feel hot and on high alert. A friendly waitress walked them back to where her father was sitting. He was at the table, with a purple bag that had a single balloon tied to it, holding a Coke in his hand. He smiled the same broad smile as Lana, and they mirrored the same toothy grin. He stood up quickly as they approached him, which seemed odd to Lana. His jumpy nature somehow felt familiar, like she had seen him before. Yet, as soon as he spoke, that feeling quickly faded.

"Hi Lana, it's so good to see you. I can't believe how big you are. I'm so happy to see you," he said.

Without a moment's hesitation, she said, "Hi Dad. I'm so happy you're here." She hugged him tightly, wanting to cry, but she held it back. As soon as they embraced, she again noticed how familiar it felt, yet she quickly fell right back to being in absolute amazement to finally be with her father.

He couldn't believe how open she was to him, so easily and readily accepting. He was grateful but felt unworthy of this. "I know I haven't been around, and it kills me that I haven't been here to see you grow. I'm really sorry it's taken me so long to get to you. I hope you can forgive me. I know

I've missed a lot of birthdays, so I got you a little gift and a card." He handed her the bag with a card that said, *"Happy Birthday to my courageous daughter."* He signed it, *"Love Always, Your Father."* Inside the bag was a history book and a colorful woven shirt.

"Thank you; it's okay. I'm just glad you're here now." She didn't really care for an explanation, she just wanted her dad, and right now, she had him right in front of her. It was a miracle; another one of her intentions had come true.

"I owe you an explanation. You see, I went on a trip from Central America to South America. I started in Guatemala, where I am originally from, and then I just went further and further south. The further I went, the harder it was for me to consider coming back to the States. I was trying to find myself, but I was really just getting more and more lost in the jungle. I just wasn't ready to come back until a couple of weeks ago. The truth is, I needed to come back to see a doctor after drinking bad water and getting parasites, so I need to get healthy before exploring again." He paused and grabbed Lana's hands. "That's when I realized I needed to see you, too. I'm sorry I've been so selfish. I've always thought about you and prayed for you. I hope you can forgive me and accept me for who I am. I'm not perfect, but I want to help you in any way I can—in my own way."

Lana's mother had kept quiet the entire time but interrupted. "She doesn't need your help. She's a straight-A student and doing very well, actually. She just needs her parents like all children do."

He nodded. "I understand," he said, looking out of the window. "I'm so glad to know that you're so accomplished and can take care of yourself. I don't know about you, but I loved learning about history in school."

"I love history, too." said Lana.

"But then I realized how much was left unsaid or even completely distorted," her father continued. "There is so much darkness in this world, Lana. One day you'll see how pain creates so much darkness..." Trailing off, he looked at Rachel with sadness. "Did you know that I left Guatemala with my mother during the civil war? I was only five, but I remember the Shadow clearly. It was an Indigenous genocide. Manic soldiers taking life in the name of religion. There is deep darkness that needs to be acknowledged."

Rachel interrupted, "And until then, we can talk about something a little more age appropriate."

"Sure," Ray nodded, looking at Lana. Slightly overwhelmed, Lana was wide-eyed and smiled awkwardly.

Lana talked about school and her accomplishments in her favorite classes. They talked about how they both liked to read books, laughing about how they had the same loud laugh and sense of humor. Lana was so much like her father, and she loved it. It made her feel proud to be like him. They talked on and on, as they both enjoyed chatting. But it was getting dark and time for them to separate. In between his travels, he said, he occasionally lived in the big city near them, and he said he'd come to visit her soon, adding that until then, they could write to each other. Lana's mother listened patiently and was reluctantly happy that they had finally met.

They parted ways and he promised to stay in touch. Lana smiled and nodded, yet as soon as he left, she felt a rush of insecurity and uncertainty flow through her. It was a strange and confusing way to feel about someone you admired and longed for. It would be weeks of mixed emotions until she finally got a letter from him. It read:

Dear Lana,

I hope you've been well. I'm sorry it's taken me so long to write to you. I wanted to say that I really enjoyed our time together the last time I saw you. I am so proud of you and how well you're doing. I wish to be someone you can be proud of. I wish I could tell you that I also did very well in school, but that isn't the truth. I had a tough childhood and had only been lucky enough to date your mother in high school for a brief time. But besides that, I haven't had an easy life.

Your mother didn't know much about me, but you see, my mama was an immigrant from Guatemala. She raised me as a single parent who fought to find work and support us. We've struggled a lot in this life. And although I loved books and learning, I had a hard time being a normal student and always felt different than the other kids. I never graduated from school, and so I work temporary jobs. That's why I go to South and Central America where it's less expensive and I feel accepted to explore and be myself. It has been tough to feel comfortable when I don't always feel safe or supported to live out my purpose. I guess I feel like I'm not good enough to be your father and that I might be a disturbance to you. I know you will always be safe within yourself. I understand that, and yet I haven't fully grasped that in my own life.

I know this is a long letter, and I've rambled a bit, but I also know how smart you are and how you will understand. See, I still don't have my life together, but I am feeling healthy and ready for an adventure. I'm always looking for something, and until I have it, I don't want to interrupt your life with my inadequacies. I am leaving this weekend, so don't write me back. I will call out to you from somewhere in the jungles, but I just wanted you to know that I love you, and I am so proud of you.

Love Always,

Your Father

P.S. Say hello to your mother and Nana for me. They have done such a good job raising you. I am thankful for that.

Lana read this letter over and over again, hoping she'd find a treasure within it that would deliver her father back to her sooner. The hard truth was that was all, and once again, she felt abandoned by him. She didn't understand why he had to come to visit her if he was just going to leave her again.

That would be the last time she'd receive a letter from him. Heartbroken all over again, she'd eventually stop thinking of him at all and soon detached from her fantasy of having a father who understood her. Unable to understand his decisions, she decided she was fine before him and would be fine without him once again. This is what she told herself, allowing her heart to harden. A dark and thicker wall rose high to keep her safely secure within it, like often happens after the heart breaks.

At this point in her young life, Lana had finally forgotten that she was pure love, a magical creation made with pure intention. Until that truth would return to her, she would unwittingly cover up her confusion with numbing and thoughtless activities, unaware of the inner shifts that were taking place. The human experience isn't an easy one, and she was feeling the inevitable darkness.

Throughout this time, the Shadows suffocated Lana's

magic until it was completely lost within her. During these dark times, she lost connection to her magic, to the elements, and to Pachamama. It was as if her golden wings separated from her body and her soul had completely flown away.

One eerie eve, when the full moon was high and the fog rolled in to cover their little home, Lana felt a displeasure in her chest and a pestering need to take off her once-beloved necklace. Trancelike, she slowly reached around for the clasp, took it off without daring to look at it, and placed it into the petrified jasper wooden box. She slipped it underneath her bed where she had other hidden treasures from her childhood, where they stayed to be forgotten and gather dust.

Over the years, Lana gradually became more aware of the pain and the darkness that existed in the world and her walls grew higher still. Unknowingly consumed by fears and shadows, she distracted herself by putting all her efforts on achievements outside herself.

Lana sensed the dark and light so intensely—she had always felt both deeply at such a tender age. All in divine timing, she would learn how to revive the light within her to illuminate the darkness. Even though she had let her wings fall and was now completely disconnected from her sacred necklace, it was destiny for her to find her own way, learning how to embrace the fullness of life as a human being. Forgetting how to express love, Lana let the Shadows overtake her rather than embracing them, too. Unbeknownst to her, that was why the Shadows crept in and pressed against her so fiercely. All things in life are seeking to be loved or give love. Forgetting this, walls of self-defense weighed heavily in her mind and hurt her heart. That is until…

The Calling

After many years of living in these shadows, Lana became accustomed to the dark. With her magic so repressed, she evolved into something entirely different from who she really was. She was profoundly disconnected from her innocence and determined to succeed in all things possible.

She didn't know who she was anymore or what she really wanted, but she knew how to get lost in her work and focus on her goals. In this way, she became successful in her career, yet she was unconscious, lost, indifferent to love, and blind to true joy. This was the definition of success that Rachel had so badly strived for and what was accepted in the so-called advanced society she now lived in.

Lana was only twenty-one years old when she had accomplished all the things she thought would make her and her mother happy. She graduated from a great college, got a good job, a nice apartment in the city, and had the perfect boyfriend, yet she wasn't truly happy. When alone, she sensed a deep nagging dissatisfaction in the pit of her stomach. She was beginning to recognize that something was very wrong. She was drowning in the darkness, and there did not seem to be any solid ground to stand on.

She'd often find herself sitting at a fancy dinner in the loud city with her friends or boyfriend, gossiping and having empty conversations, feeling the depths of how shallow her life was. She began to see how lonely she was surrounded by people who felt like complete strangers. Lana felt like she was actually drowning in water. She was lost and alone in depths of disconnection while living in the shallow end of life. Extravagance and frills could only partially mask the emptiness. However, in moments of grace, she could sense that something existed which was more authentic than what she could see directly in front of her. She had a clarity that seemed out of grasp, yet it was so real and painful to feel. She felt a deep heartache in the midst of what she was experiencing and the lifestyle she was living.

At her twenty-second birthday dinner, as she blew out the candles on her gourmet chocolate cake, someone handed her a birthday bag with a purple balloon. Something stirred deeply within her, remembering her father's gift. Once again, she realized that she was a missing part of herself; a part of herself to embrace and no longer resent. Being given such a similar gift was a divine synchronicity that painfully reminded her of her child-self and her father. However, it landed heavily in her heart, and she was suffocating in the realization that something was very wrong. Feeling lost and unable to express what she felt, she knew she needed to make a change within herself. It started and ended with her.

Fully feeling this pain was the first step to take before she could act. Although it was difficult to acknowledge, Lana was lighter in her soul from recognizing and accepting the emotions she felt. She had just hit rock bottom, yet these inner shifts were forming necessary change.

That night, she began to have an intensely realistic dream where she wandered through a dense jungle. She followed a small dirt path that wound and weaved without rhyme or reason. Climbing over vines and low-hanging branches, she began to make out a clearing ahead of her. Silently stepping into the space, she saw a rugged man lightly touching the surrounding plants. He paused to hug a tree, which seemed so odd—seeing another person, especially a man, doing what she only knew herself to do.

The moment he opened his mouth and spoke, Lana knew she was watching her father. "This is the Earth Mother, Pachamama, your oldest ancient ancestor. She is part of you and always here, living and present in these lands of magic." Looking over his shoulder, straight into her eyes, he said, "And you, Lana Livia, are the last in line with your ancestral magic."

Lana covered her mouth in utter shock from seeing her father connecting with Pachamama. They were one in the same and Lana could clearly see her fathers love for their Earth Mother.

Ray stepped away from the trees, sitting down by a creek bed with his expression darkening. "But the Shadow is growing stronger throughout the world, suffocating the magic through the choices we make to connect or move farther away."

Lana gulped and sat wide-eyed from such intense revelations.

"Don't be afraid! I'm sorry, I startled you—let's dance!" Ray hummed a familiar song, and together by the creek, they swayed in sweet harmony.

Lana woke herself by singing in her sleep.

"I used to go out to parties

And stand around

'Cause I was too nervous

To really get down

But my body yearned to be free..."

Lana awoke, holding her own hands, feeling a tear stream down her cheek. It all felt so real, more true than the world she woke back up to. Several moments passed, and she relished being in the dreamy state where magic still takes place. Holding herself tightly, she drifted back into a dreamless, deep sleep.

When she awoke the next morning, she felt a new kind of comfort open within her heart. While the dream filled her with emotions, she felt it was better to know of the truth and feel its love than to not be aware of it at all.

Shifts and Synchronicities

A couple of days later, on what seemed like an ordinary day, Lana decided to get some exercise before going home after work. As she was walking to the gym, a cold breeze brought with it a dewy fog that blanketed the drab city. Lana shivered as she walked through the dark mist. When she arrived at the gym, she was late to her regular class, so she decided to try yoga. She hadn't tried yoga before, but she had heard it was a good workout.

Lana sat on a provided mat, anxious to begin, when a radiant yoga teacher walked in. Just like the sun shining to greet the day, the teacher introduced herself to the class as Sunny. She explained that she was the substitute today, so the class would be a little different from what they might be used to.

Sunny first guided them through a breathing session and explained, "By bringing attention to the breath, we can bring attention to the present moment. Most people don't know how to breathe properly, and they breathe shallowly without nourishing their bodies. However, by taking big belly breaths we can help cleanse and heal the body temple."

They were then guided through a gentle meditation where for a fleeting moment, Lana remembered her inner-self glowing. As they progressed into the practice, instead of a vigorous workout like Lana was used to, they did a restorative flow that was calming and nourishing. They then closed the class with a chant of *"Om."* Sunny then spoke, sharing something that resonated with Lana. "The light within me honors the light within you." This statement touched her, flooding her with memories of childhood when she felt her magic and golden wings. After the class, she waited till the last person left so she could speak with Sunny.

"I have to ask, where are you from? And how can I learn to be more like you?" Lana asked, laughing timidly.

"Well thank you. I appreciate you seeing me. Most of all, I am a reflection of who you really are." Sunny paused so Lana could sit with that for a moment and then continued slowly. "I live locally, but I travel a lot, because I like to visit sacred places and mindful communities where my spirit can flourish and expand. Sometimes in the city it is difficult to be still and listen. Yet, that is the grand challenge to integrate the beautiful experiences we have had. I think you would benefit from coming to Bali next month to see and feel what I mean. My yoga retreat can help you strengthen your practice."

Lana partially understood what was said. She replied, "Thank you for the invitation, but that would be impossible. My work doesn't give me any breathing room." Sunny's eyes got larger at the words "breathing room," and Lana was too stunned by the experience to actually voice the intense "yes" that she felt inside her. Being disconnected from her light, just as Pachamama had foretold, made it nearly impossible to listen to her inner self. This experience shook her out of her slumber just for a moment, yet one sacred pause to be present was long enough to make a deep, meaningful shift within her.

The experience at Sunny's yoga class brought up a memory from Lana's childhood. She was reminded of a time when she heard the Fire's song. It seemed so long ago, but she remembered a slight feeling of wonder, expansiveness, and lightness. And her wings! She was faintly glowing, trying to remember the words the Fire had sung, when she was interrupted by her phone ringing. It was her boyfriend, Sam, asking her to bring home some take-out from their favorite place.

Sam greeted her with a kiss on the cheek, grabbed his food, and headed to the sofa to eat in front of the television. Lana wasn't very hungry. She was lost in her thoughts, dreaming of yoga and Bali. She hadn't taken a vacation since she started working with her company two years ago. Instead, she liked cashing in on her vacation hours to make more money so she could watch her bank account grow and her student loan balance drop. She always thought she loved being super busy; never lazy, never still. Yet the memory of Sunny, who was brimming with iridescence even in the modern world, had inspired constant daydreams of what a couple of weeks of yoga in Bali would feel like. And just like that, a small shift and a divine synchronicity made ripples throughout Lana's whole being.

A week later, she found herself researching Bali and saw that flights were affordable. In a moment of beauty and faith, she booked her trip on a whim. She felt excited and nervous because she had never traveled outside of the States! This was going to be something big, and she could feel it deep in her heart.

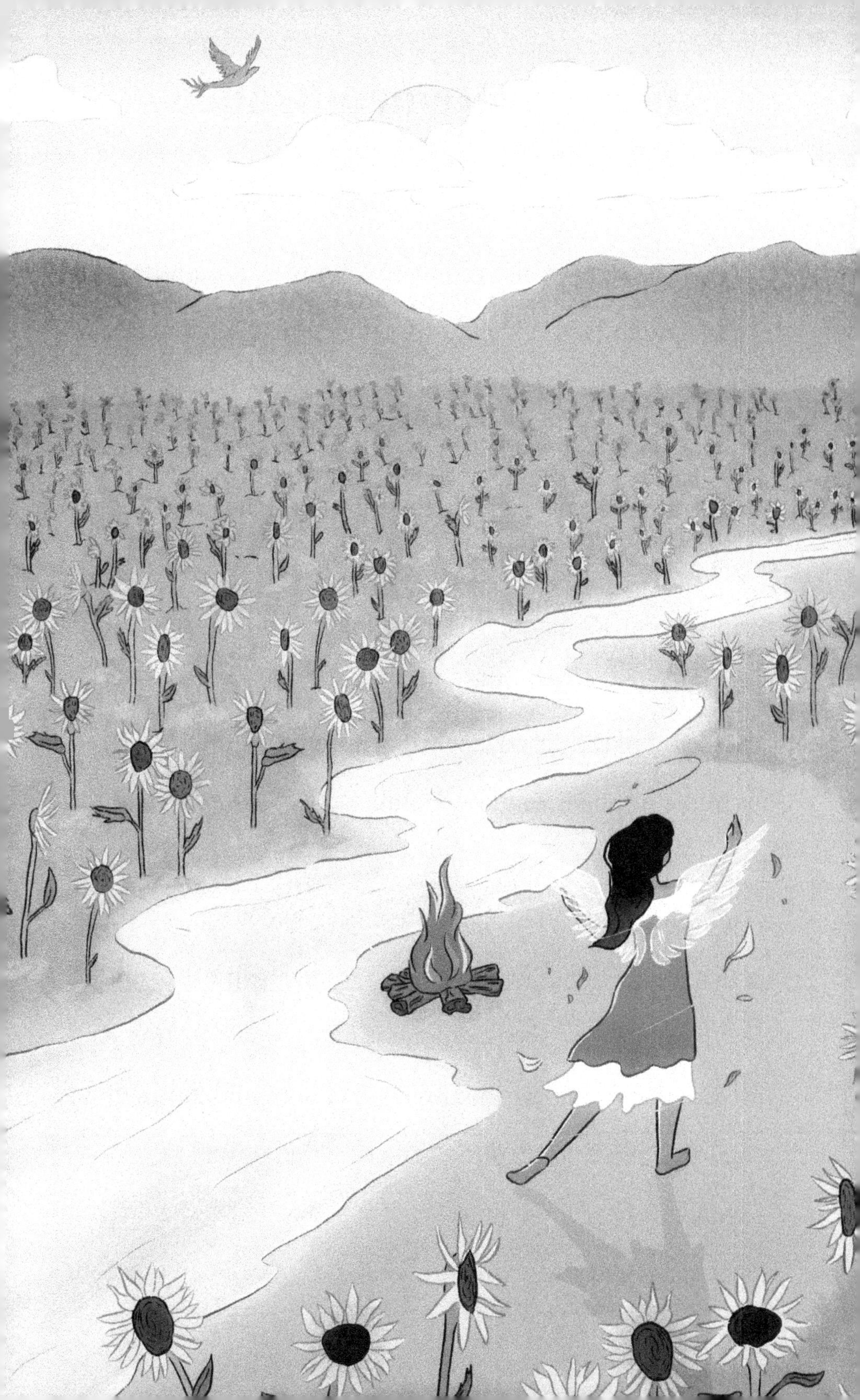

Oasis of Remembrance

Lana looked out the airplane window with amazement as she flew to Bali, the land of paradise. Daydreaming and occasionally dozing off, she kept slipping into the most familiar place. She kept dreaming that she was on a quest, making her way through a desert. She was headed to what seemed like an oasis where she was always filled with curiosity and adventure. She remembered how supportive it felt to be there. Yet, in this particular dream, right before she made it out of the desert, she woke up and saw the vast ocean out of the airplane window. Being so sleepy, it was hard for her to completely remember what she was dreaming and which parts were real memories. She knew that by being on that plane and going on a quest to reach an oasis, all felt very familiar, like she had done it many times before. And just like that, Lana was taking her and her childhood self on a real-life quest, headed to a land of paradise and bliss.

Intuitively, she would feel more supported if she arrived a few days early to explore and settle into the area before she began a new daily regimen. As she left the airport and ventured to the retreat, she quickly realized she was in the most magical city she had ever been to! It was unlike anything she had ever imagined was possible in the world she normally lived in. Here there was lush greenery and sprawling rice fields surrounded by the jungle. It was paradise. In the small city on every corner were magical shops with jewelry, art, and the most mysterious stones. She also began to eat the best food she'd ever had. Lana wasn't a vegan, but since vegan cafés were plentiful and incredible, she decided to eat more mindfully, and her body thanked her for it. She felt her morning lethargy lift and her complexion brighten. Over those few days, she wandered all over the city. She even made her way deep into the jungle. She felt grounded, refreshed, present, and peaceful.

On the day before the retreat began, while exploring, she came across something that called out to her heart. Most of the homes she saw looked like elaborate temples with rich colors, decorated with majestic art, and this one was no exception. In the front of the temple-home was a large statue of Ganesh, an elephant-headed deity, who she later learned was the remover of obstacles and the lord of success. Lana was taken aback by the whole scene as she then saw a woman coming to her wearing an ornate dress and warm smile. She gestured for Lana to sit in front of her, introducing herself as Gede.

"How can I support you, child?" asked Gede.

"I stopped to look at the statue, and then I read your sign. I've never been to a healer before so I'm curious to learn about you and the statue. Also, the couple that I saw leaving looked so refreshed and inspired. Is there anything you can tell me to help me with my life?" said Lana.

"I honor you following your curious heart and coming into this space, dear child. You have everything you need inside. You get to listen and remember who you really are," said Gede, eating a bright purple dragon fruit. She continued, "and yet, you have many shadows surrounding you, seeking to be seen. For now, feel into the pleasure that comes from being in paradise, living in your bliss. Glimpse what life is like outside the haze of the busy world. Let peace wash over your soul while you remember what life alive feels like," said Gede. "I must go now, it is time for me to rest.

I was supposed to be done for the day after the couple, yet I felt your calling. May your shadows be embraced, your obstacles removed, and your gifts be remembered. Good luck."

Lana wasn't sure she fully understood what had been shared, but she felt uplifted after speaking with Gede. She walked away in a tranquil state, pondering the conversation as her heart began to slowly crack back open.

The next day, Lana began her yoga retreat with Sunny and found it to be relaxing but quite structured. They practiced meditation and gentle yoga first thing in the morning, followed by a light and healthy breakfast. Then there were more vigorous yoga classes, then lunch. Next was a ceremony in the afternoon, in which the students went into a meditative, intentional, and reflective state. The evening was for stillness and integration of the day's lessons, followed by dinner. Then they closed the day with cleansing and gratitude. It was a bit overwhelming for Lana yet she did her best to remain grateful for the experience. She had never been in a place that asked for so much patience and presence. It felt like work, but not the kind of work she was used to performing in schooling or a career.

During the first afternoon ceremony, they all sat together in a circle for the ritual. Sunny guided them to close their eyes, breathe into the moment, and ground into the earth.

"Without alcohol, caffeine, TV or any other numbing devices, you will notice that you start to feel more deeply. You will become more sensitive. In this way, you can allow your heart to expand. Give yourself permission to feel into nature, the faith-driven locals, the supportive community surrounding us, and this peaceful space of love that is abundant and is for all," guided Sunny.

Sunny also mentioned that there was a New Moon, so they would be having a fire ceremony later that night. She invited them to remember that it was a powerful time to set intentions. She continued, "We will each write in our journals all the things we wish to let go of and once we're done writing, we'll tear the pages out and burn them in the fire. In this way, we can transform the power of those old stories and like the Phoenix, rise up in love."

This was a powerful opening night for the retreat, and Lana felt like she'd freed herself from some of the weight that she had been carrying on her shoulders. As she watched the flames flickering, yet another memory from her childhood came back to her. Lana saw herself flying out of her burning childhood home, her wings lifting her to safety. She remembered how the Fire sang to her something about pausing to find peace. Feeling the direct similarity to what she was now experiencing in Bali, Lana began to realize how it was like all those moments were preparing her for her current life! She stood in awe as the transformative fires were once again making room for her golden wings. She began to open back up to her truth by remembering all the times she had experienced this kind of bliss as a child by living in her magic!

Every day was extraordinary in its own way. Filled with quiet, peace, and powerful movement she felt so much expansion. Lana laughed, sang, and cried like she had never before. She recognized that she was feeling fully alive for the first time since she was a child by experiencing a direct connection to the magical world with the paradise she was now experiencing.

On the last day, she was feeling especially sensitive

and receptive. The closing of the retreat included a cacao ceremony with Mayan cacao from Guatemala. This felt so familiar to Lana, and she remembered that is where her ancestors were from. Sunny introduced them to this plant medicine at the end of the retreat to assist them in deeply feeling all that had taken place. She also shared that it would assist them in being open to carry the magic with them as they went their separate ways.

Sunny said, "With our cups of cacao next to our hearts, we can set our intentions. I'd like to go around the circle and ask each of you to share aloud what your intentions are. After that, I will begin to play the drum and I invite you to go on a journey, guided by your sacred heart, remaining open to any wisdom or guidance that comes through."

When it came time for Lana to speak her truth, she took a deep breath and spoke. "My intention is to stay lovingly open and I want to remember." Making her intention known, Lana laid down, and hearing the beating drum, she felt her whole body vibrate. She began to feel her body expand wide open as she entered into a majestic, enchanted forest.

Lana squished her toes into the moss and rubbed her hands

across the sprawling ferns that softly blanketed the forest floor. She somewhat remembered the feeling, yet something wasn't quite the same. Looking out into the forest, she could see a friend sitting at the base of a tree. It was Felix the Fox! In full amazement, Lana ran over to him, yet he said nothing. With a swift flash, he dove through a doorway hidden in the tree trunk. Instinctively, she followed, rubbing her hand across the bark as she did. Instantly, she was flooded with memories of an ancient oak, fairies, songs of love, and a gift given to her by the mother of the forest.

As she entered through the doorway, she was sent into another world with sunflowers stretching out as far as the eyes could see. She looked around for her guide, but Felix was nowhere to be seen. Turning instead to greet the sunflowers, a breeze brushed her cheek. Smiling, she remembered that she had been here before. Lana exhaled fully, her breath an offering to the element of Air. She could feel her whole soul softening as if she had just returned to the home she always knew was there yet forgot the way back.

Looking to her left, the swaying sunflowers melted into a shimmering river. Lana ran over to the water's edge and jumped in without hesitation. Instantly, she felt her spirit shine throughout the waters, turning into blissful bioluminescence. Feeling cleansed and clear, she glided out of the waters, shifting her focus onto a fire that burned brightly amongst some rocks. Lana held out her hands to feel the flames as it instantly dried and warmed her radiant body. The Fire sparked with joy to once again be seen and felt by a child of magic.

Softened by the Air, cleansed by the Sea, and warmed by the Fire, Lana felt her feet reaching deeply and grounding into the Earth. There she stood, a perfectly clear channel, divinely aligned with the sacred elements. Closing her eyes, Lana heard a familiar voice speak to her heart. *"You will return. All in divine timing."*

Lana opened her eyes and looked around. She was still surrounded by sunflowers, the sacred waters, and could feel the fire's warmth, yet something had just shifted. Softly, she walked back to the water and peered over the edge to see her reflection. Reflected back was herself, yet now she was five years old with the most radiant, golden wings that any being had ever been bestowed.

The remembrance of her magic ignited the Fire and rising out of the flames blossomed the most majestic Phoenix. Rising from the ashes and ascending into full expansion, the Phoenix transformed into a Hummingbird. Lighting up the whole enchanted land with their radiance, Lana and the Hummingbird lifted up into flight. They danced through the sky, joining together in a sacred, magical union. They soared up through the sky and swooped down past waterfalls and majestic mountains, grazing the tips of the sea of sunflowers.

They headed to the center of the field where a familiar flower glowed with absolute vibrance. Inside the flower lay the most peculiar item! It was a tiny glass jar filled with shimmering stardust and a single cacao bean. Lana immediately recognized it as a piece of her necklace and was flooded with full remembrance of her magic. Reaching out to feel the flower and retrieve her gift, the flower released a mist of pure magic that washed over the whole land, igniting it into full ecstasy. The sunflowers lifted high into the sky, singing as they swayed.

"We are loved, we are related in the light.

You are loved, you are the light.

Swing this way, let us remind you of your ways.

Sweet as the sun, Magic child we are one."

Lana lowered her face closer to the flower and she began to see a familiar face shining through. Pachamama bloomed through the flower of magic and once again, as she had promised, presented herself to Lana:

"You have remembered what your magic feels like,

What wonder and amazement smells like.

What being connected to all looks like.

Welcome home, dear child.

And yet, your journey is just beginning."

In the blink of an eye, Pachamama morphed out of her radiant form and into the sleekest, most majestic black jaguar. Stunned and startled, Lana exclaimed, "What? Who are you?"

This time, the jaguar leaped towards her and growled softly, "Your ancestors are calling for you! Remember!" And in a flash, he leapt away again.

Completely taken aback, Lana gasped and started running back to the tree that she had entered this world from. She could feel the Shadows chasing her, and because she was desperate for help, Felix appeared to guide her safely back into her body. She was shaken, yet she held firmly onto her gift. It was her token of remembrance and it remained fully intact.

Clearing Out the Fog

Lana took a deep breath in and felt her body resting on the ground. She could hear Sunny speaking, "Remember to breathe deeply and return softly. Wherever you went, remember where you are in this now moment. Wiggling your hands and toes, bring feeling back to the body. When you're ready, roll to your side and remember you are safe and you are loved."

Coming back into her body, Lana was wholly inspired and in complete remembrance. She was a child of magic, miraculous and extraordinary as she had ever been, and once again, she was closely connected to her truth. While she lay there in the bliss of this remembrance, slowly her perspective began to shift and she could see a bigger picture than all things being purely pleasant. She remembered that she had a life back in the big city, a boyfriend who she felt so distant from, and unhealed pains that lingered, tethered to her heart. Brimming with emotion, the words of the healer Gede came back to her and now, she understood them fully:

"You have everything you need inside you. You get to listen and remember who you really are. And yet, you have many shadows surrounding you, seeking to be seen."

Lana sat up softly, recognizing she had work to do and also much more to discover. In the midst of this new-found clarity, one thing was especially clear. By following her curious heart and coming to the retreat, she had remembered her magic and had been shown what shadows surrounded her. She could now answer the call and go to the land of her ancestors. The jaguar was her messenger and she was able to listen, trusting her heart.

Lana remembered that her father was from Guatemala, and yet she hadn't seen him or heard from him in many years. She didn't fully understand why she felt she must go there, yet she knew it would serve her well to trust. Even though most of her life she was not empowered to trust her heart, she felt secure in her knowing. It was like she was waiting for permission from herself, and so now, after finally taking steps to climb out of the fog of the world, she felt grounded and clear.

On the plane home she journaled as she flew, writing

down a realization:

"This trip to Bali was merely the first step in a much bigger quest. Everything really does happen in divine timing. Sunny inspired me to visit Bali, and now Bali is leading me to Guatemala. I see that all things are happening for me, not to me. It has always been this way, and now I remember! I am receptive and ready to really listen."

The moment she got back home, Lana decided to open up to her boyfriend immediately. Sam was sitting on the couch watching a sports game, eating noodles, and barely paying her mind when she broke the news.

"Sam, I have to talk to you. I've never felt fully at home here in the big city and I don't think you even know me. Often when I'm with you and our friends, I've felt so lonely and lost." She paused to find the courage to continue. "And that's not your fault, it's mine. I must answer this call and find myself. I need to learn how to love myself before I can love another person. I don't really even know what exactly it is that I'm looking for. Yet I know I have to go or the Shadows will suffocate me here."

Sam was surprised by her revelation. He thought

everything about their life was perfectly fine. It was difficult for him to see why she would want to leave it all behind. He thought Lana's spontaneous trip to Bali was a strange fluke and didn't seek to understand what a calling meant.

"I don't understand where this is all coming from. You met someone in Bali, is that it?"

Hearing his insecurity, Lana calmly responded, "No, Sam. That's not what this is about at all. In fact, this isn't really even about you. It's about me. That might sound selfish, but how can I give myself to you if I feel incomplete and don't even know what I want?" Lana knew this was blunt yet she knew she was being called to express herself openly. "I'm doing this for me and even though it's a big surprise for you, I hope you can trust and be okay with that."

"I just don't get you," stammered Sam.

"Neither do I, and that's exactly the point. I'm sorry Sam. I don't want to hurt you, but it is clear. I have to go," said Lana.

Sam was upset. He hated change but knew there was no point in arguing with Lana for too long. She was strong willed and would have it her way in the end. This wasn't easy for Lana by any means. She felt guilty for hurting him. However, she knew these were the shadows that must be faced with love so she could continue on her divine path of discovering her destiny.

Led by her heart, she packed her things quickly before she could change her mind. Sensing the major shifts Lana was allowing to take place, Pachamama lovingly watched, ready to witness magical transformation. Singing out to her through the whispering winds, Pachamama soothed Lana's tender heart:

"In this reality, it is no wonder why so many forget how to believe in their magic. But suffering and pain are our teachers, there to reveal to us our oneness. Showing us how similar our ailments are and how we're all connected as the same. Fear not, for if you listen closely, you will hear my calling. We are always here to guide you, back to your heart."

Lana listened as she gathered all her belongings, releasing all things she wouldn't need any longer. What no longer served her was out. The wind blew inside the room and the breeze touched her skin, sending shivers up her spine. She was on the right path and her truth would light up her path with a glow that warmed her heart.

Pachamama continued, *"You have been shaken out of the fog, long enough to feel and listen. You are gifted with remembering. You will next experience what your magic felt like. What childlike wonder smelled like. What being connected to all looked like. Once more, you will come back into your magical knowing."*

Lana left the apartment, never to look back at the person or the home she left behind. That phase was not intended to last for too long. With her possessions inside a suitcase and a backpack, she jumped into a taxi and headed directly for the airport. She took a deep breath, and she noticed a glimmer of magical dust that shimmered on her bags.

After many heartaches and hard lessons, she was coming into full awareness, ready for the journey of discovery. She felt an urgency to connect with the indigenous land in Guatemala, with her ancestors, and with her untethered magic once again. It was time to fly away from that which made her feel lost and lonely so she could see her truth more clearly.

She was apprehensive yet filled with enthusiasm as she arrived at the airport. Even though it was full of people dashing hectically, it seemed alive, welcoming, and beautifully vibrant. Lana walked through the terminal, sensing the colorful fairies that gathered to light up her path. It was a place for flight and expansion and Lana was fully prepared for the journey ahead. She hopped on the plane with a one-way ticket to growth!

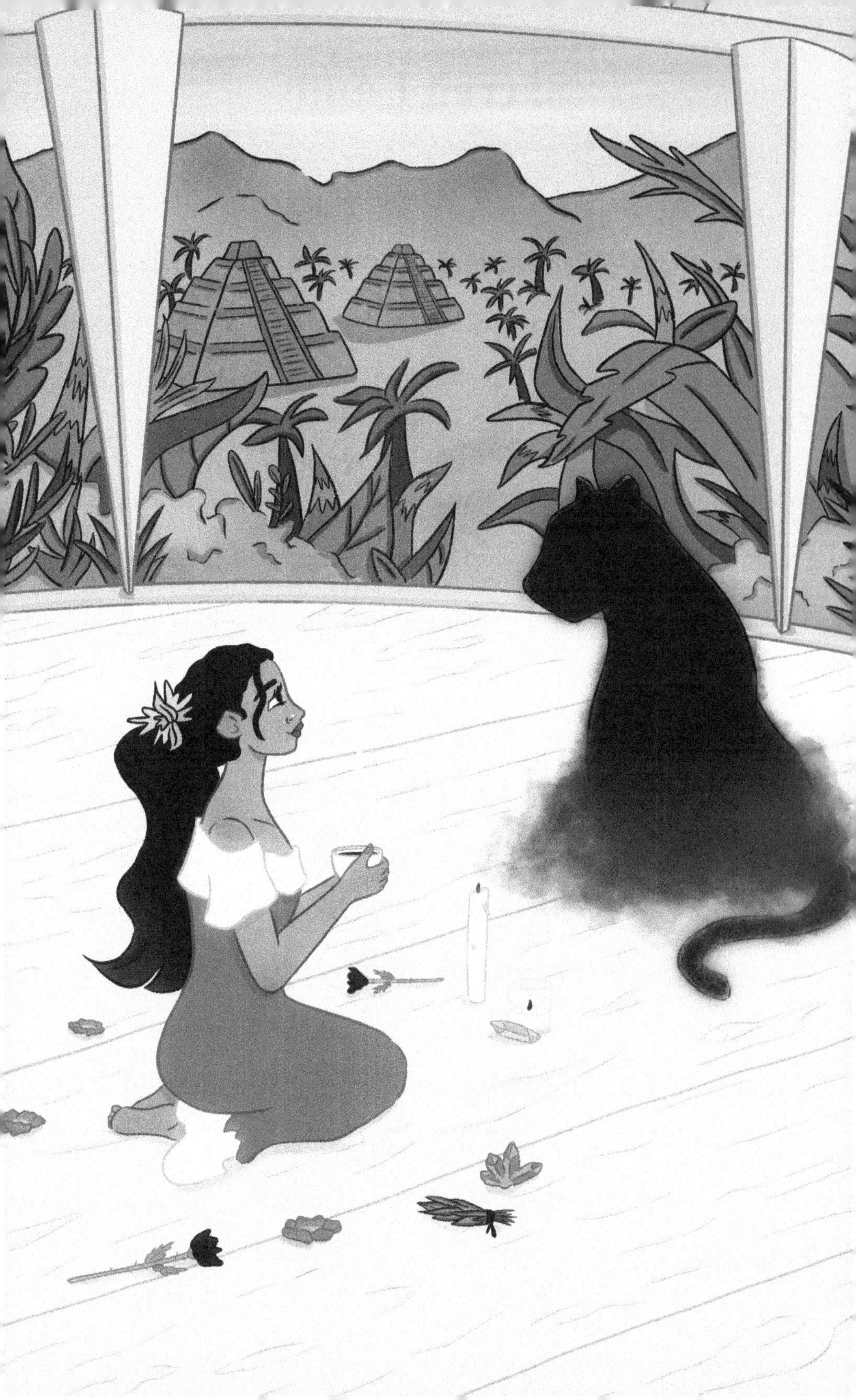

Sacred Lands

Stepping off the airplane and back onto the land of her ancestors, Lana felt the warmth envelop her like a comforting blanket. She looked up to the sky, feeling the sun shining its blessings onto her whole body. While enraptured in familiarity, she also realized that she was in a completely new land with so much to discover. She hadn't made any specific plans and was trusting the magic to guide her exactly wherever she needed to go.

Lana collected her bags and stepped outside to greet the world she'd found herself in. At first glance, she felt dismayed by the city and chaotic traffic dashing about in a frenzy. She began to become worried she made a naive mistake by not making any plans, yet she believed that somehow things would work out. She remembered how the last time that she went on a journey, Felix appeared to guide her exactly where she was destined to go! She saw a patch of grass and freshly budding flowers, so she sat down amongst the greenery.

Shifting out of fear and into her heart, Lana called out to her furry friend. "Felix, I know this may seem crazy, but I need your help. You have always been there for me and now I need you more than…"

Before she could even finish, Felix dashed around the bushes and jumped into her lap! She was ecstatic and hugged him tightly. "Oh Felix, you're here!"

"I am always here for you Lana, I am indeed a guide but I am here to direct you in the way you're already going," Felix comforted her.

Lana was still anxious, "Well, where is that? What am I doing here in this land now? Remember after I followed you in the journey I saw the jaguar? I want to pick up where we left off, when he told me that my ancestors were calling and to remember something."

Sensing her worry, Felix soothed her by brushing his tail against her cheek. She softened and felt a tingle in her heart. Letting out a big, loud sigh, Lana returned back home to herself. As she let go of trying to figure out the meaning of it all, it was as if her hands were opening to receive something else. By letting go, she received exactly what she needed. It truly was inside her all along.

"It's the jar with the cacao bean," she exclaimed! "That's it! That's what was laying in the flower during our last journey. I remember! Felix, could you be so kind as to guide me to where I can see cacao being grown and used?"

"I would be honored to the utmost!"

Following Felix's lead, Lana dashed through the bushes and once again, found herself in a majestic land. Except this time, it wasn't a vision; it was the real world, yet entirely magical! They arrived in the midst of a lush landscape where volcanoes, groves of trees, deep shimmering waters, and quaint villages were scattered about. Lana rested her hand on her heart, and still feeling some doubt about whether or not she was actually seeing this, blinked hard and fast.

"Oh you funny human, I love you so. Don't you see! As a child, you saw these places of magic with your innocence. Now, you are seeing how the world really is when you follow your heart. Your time to experience your destiny is arriving. You will need strength for what is ahead. You will be scared at times, and so remember that is okay too; the trick is to simply not believe in the fear and stay in your sacred heart.

You are expanding with each courageous breath you take."

As always, with a dash, Felix was gone, leaving Lana standing tall and prepared for the discovery ahead.

Wandering down into the village below, Lana felt like she was back in her childhood backyard. She was on a quest toward a sacred place that would provide a haven for her soul and answers to her greatest curiosities. Moving through the streets and pathways, she absorbed it all fully, feeling it rekindling a fire that lay waiting. Growing tired from such excitement and expansion, she looked for a place to nest and settle in. She quickly found a place that felt like home to her.

"Welcome to Casa Alegria! Do you have a room yet or have you just now wandered in?" asked a cheery gentleman.

"Hi, and thank you," Lana said softly. "I am Lana and I just arrived here. I'm just going with the flow! Do you have a place for me?"

"Okay, Lana. I'm Dan, and your room can be over here," he offered, pointing to a small bungalow. It was perfectly placed next to an open space where there were yoga mats, instruments, and drums. "That bungalow is all for you, and the kitchen over here is shared. There is a shala down below, close to the water where the view is amazing."

"Incredible; it all looks perfect," said Lana.

Dan guided Lana through the place and mentioned that many animals and pets roamed around freely, so she should keep an eye on where she stepped or sat. He introduced her to some of the furry friends that were around and then they walked down to the shala. "And these human friends over here are amazing as well," he bellowed. "Alice and Sheila, this is Lana!"

"Hi! Welcome," said Sheila and Alice in unison. With genuine, shimmering smiles, they all hugged like reunited friends.

"Where are you from?" asked Sheila.

"I'm from California."

"And how long will you be staying here?" asked Alice.

"Umm, I don't know yet," said Lana. "I booked a one-way ticket with my intuition and am here to learn."

"The best way to do it. Going with the flow, seeing what feels right," said Alice.

"Listening to your intuition always leads to the best discoveries," said Sheila. "And you know what? You could join us for a cacao ceremony at sunset since you don't have any plans! It's the perfect way to begin any adventure."

"That sounds amazing! I've been to one before, but what kind of cacao ceremony is this?" asked Lana.

The girls shared with Lana that the cacao ceremony was a gathering held to open the heart and give full reverence to the land. It would be a traditional ceremony held by an indigenous shaman and not like ones experienced in foreign lands. Lana's spine tingled when she heard that this ceremony was held in respect to her ancestors. After only being there a few minutes, she noticed how she was already being guided back to cacao once again.

"You'll love it. We'll go down to the ceremony at five, okay!" said Alice cheerfully.

The girls left to go for a swim, and Lana decided to settle in and research more about cacao. She found that cacao was the natural form that chocolate came from, yet it was pure so it retained it's antioxidants, vitamins, and minerals. Its use dated back to the ancient Aztec and Mayan times when they used it for medicinal as well as ceremonial purposes. It seemed to be as common then as coffee had now become.

Seeing how it was the foundation of her ancestors' entire way of living, she found it perplexing that she was only now learning about it. Her curiosity was piqued, and she knew she was on the right path!

Regrouping after the afternoon adventures, the three girls came together to venture to the ceremony. Feeling clean and clear, they meandered down a winding, jungle path. With each step Lana took farther into the unknown, she grew closer to her truth. Nearing the ceremony, Lana heard music that permeated her physical body and resonated with her soul. It called out to her and her spirit answered by dancing along. She followed the music with her magical friends, as they all smiled warmly and danced freely.

They were greeted by a young shaman who welcomed them sincerely with kind eyes that shined more brilliantly than a smile ever could. She had never met a shaman before and thought he'd be ancient and intimidating. On the contrary, he was young, kind, and shared feelings of safety and peace. He guided them into the site where others gathered, preparing for the ceremony.

It was expansive and spectacular, and it took Lana's

breath away. She felt dizzy with the lightness that came over her. She witnessed an eagle gliding overhead, and she instantly felt reconnected. She remembered the wings she used to imagine as a child, taking flight and glittering in the sunshine.

"Oh my," Lana managed. "This is incredible."

"I'm so happy you are here! It's all so beautiful and you haven't even tasted the cacao yet," said Alice.

Lana could stay staring into the sky and feeling her magic for forever, but she was guided to sit by the fire and join the circle of people that had gathered. Someone handed her a cup of cacao, and Lana instantly felt her heart beat faster and fuller.

"Welcome sisters, brothers," said the shaman as he took a deep breath, closing his eyes. "We bless this cacao, and we give thanks to the cacao spirit for helping us to open our hearts. We call in our ancestors who love us unconditionally, giving thanks for their support. We bless the land, maltyox to Pachamama for the bounties that give us this sacred plant ally. Come home to yourself. Allow your heart to assist you in remembering your truth."

The cacao smelled of earthy, dark chocolate, and she savored the taste as she sipped the drink slowly. It tasted chalky and bitter yet sweet and spicy, making her think of a dark chocolate bar that had been ground up and mixed with spices. "This all feels like a dream from my childhood," she reflected.

Finishing her cacao, Lana felt her spirit lift and soar. She was tapped back in and remembered she was made of infinite possibilities, one with Great Spirit, and one with all. She felt her golden inner light glowing intensely throughout her body.

"I feel so tingly," Lana whispered to Alice with eyes aglow.

"Notice whatever feels right for you," continued the shaman. "We use cacao for ceremonial, medicinal, and healing purposes. We harness this plant medicine as a gift to open and assist us in listening to our hearts, releasing that which no longer serves. You may find release through sweat, tears, or even shaking. Feel deeply and let go of expectations. Whatever insights you may have were already there, waiting to be heard by your open heart."

This revelation was precisely what Lana had desired. She nodded in reverence and smiled towards the shaman. "In these modern days, most people are cut off from their capacity to feel. You've been taught to dim your light and turn away from your feelings," continued the shaman. "We release that old story. It no longer serves you. Allow the cacao to assist you in reconnecting with your ancestors, to these lands, and your inner-self so you can feel deeply and live fully. Here in the present moment, we remember who we truly are."

Lana glowed in golden radiance brighter still. Her aura flashed a bright pink then orange, returning to a golden hue that expanded throughout the room and into the world around her. Her light stayed steady and she felt connected back to her truest self. The music got louder as the room became luminous with radiant beings, shining and dancing with open hearts.

As Lana danced, a deep darkness began to surround her! She twirled with the feelings, wishing for the darkness to go away. Yet the Shadow persisted, pressing down like a suffocating cloud. Lana remembered feeling this many times in the past. Calling out to her childhood self, she watched a young girl dash out of her own body! Holding hands to dance with each other, the child helped her move in the midst of the Shadow. They cried with joy, and Lana smiled, gazing at her sweet innocent self. It was a beautiful, powerful recognition. This was what she was looking for! She remembered the gift of the cacao bean that led her straight back into this land and into this dance with her inner child. Together they created space to be free from the oppressive Shadow, and it would never be able to suffocate her the same!

She was led to the lands of her ancestors to remember, and she was not finished. Just as Felix had said, the time to experience her destiny was arriving, and she would need courage for what was ahead. Blossomed and fully ready, Lana sent out a call to all her guides, ancestors, and divine mother Pachamama. The first to answer Lana's beacon of light was the Hummingbird. Swooping into the ceremony, he hovered over her head. Bursting into flight through the flames, he transformed into a radiant Phoenix, inspiring Lana to also lift in flight.

The Phoenix beckoned: "Your moment of recognition

has arrived. That which you have been seeking and which has been seeking you awaits. Come with me, and see all that you know yourself to be."

Without hesitation, Lana followed him deeper into the jungle. Flying into what seemed to be impenetrable darkness, their light pierced through just enough to make way for their discovery. Lana could feel doubt beginning to creep in and worried that maybe this was too much, that maybe she did not have enough light to make it out of the dark world they had just penetrated. Responding to her doubts, the Phoenix turned to Lana, imparting his last message of inspiration. "You are ready to see and fully able to feel. You are divinely prepared. You may not feel that in this moment, yet I leave you in full faith. Become who you are. Allow yourself to be transformed, seeing what awaits you on the other side of your own fears."

Surrounded by a sea of darkness, Lana felt like she could be drowning, yet she knew she stood on solid ground. Knowing that she was loved and fully supported, she let go of all fears. With eyes wide open in the deepest of all darkness, she opened her palms to the sky and planted her soles firmly on the ground. Her heart bursted open, shining in her light. She was fully open to discover what awaited on the other side. She was ready. Lana looked out into the unseen world that stretched out before her, and the only thing peering back were a pair of glistening golden yellow eyes.

"I see you and I remember you! Show yourself!" Lana commanded.

The Jaguar crept up slowly towards Lana's feet, stepping into her light. Softly he bowed his head and spoke. "Dear child, you have done so well. You have overcome so much to be here now."

"I remember seeing you my whole life!" Lana exclaimed. "You were in the forest when I was young, in my dreams, and in my visions. I feel like I have always known you, but I don't know who you really are."

"I am that which has been calling you home. I am your messenger. Through my own life, you are led and loved. I am now in the darkness, yet I am not the Shadows that have scared you. I am here for you my sweet child, for I am your Father."

Lana absorbed his words deeply into her heart. Flooded with feelings, she could not speak, yet she remained fully open.

"I know we have startled each other throughout our lives. I was never ready to show myself to you fully. And when you were younger, I wasn't ready then either. I know I have caused you much pain. It was never my desire to hurt you. This is a selfish excuse, but I had much to do in the land of my ancestors. Do you remember the letter I wrote to you? The one I sent right before I returned to these lands."

"Yes. I remember. You said you were looking for something and until you had it, you couldn't come back to me." Lana said fiercely.

"You're exactly right. I felt unworthy and wasn't ready to be your father, yet now I see how that hurt you. What I was looking for is what we all get to look for; my truest self. And I found that where you now stand. The site you are standing on is ancient, sacred land."

Lifting her eyes past her own golden aura, Lana saw she stood in the midst of towering temples and the most magnificent structures. As she looked around, each place her eyes landed, life returned to the land! Everything blossomed, vibrating with resurrected vitality as she stood in the midst of all her Mayan ancestors. She could see life being born, cacao being shared, luscious forests of food, people gathered around fires, and even many people being buried back into the ground. It was as if she had returned in the midst of all eras and was now seeing the whole history of her people lived out before her. The Jaguar, her father, had spent his life searching for these forgotten sacred sites. It was his mission to bring remembrance to these sites even though his decisions had caused her much pain. And now, his rugged body was one of those being returned to the Earth, which troubled Lana greatly.

"Why, in the midst of such beauty and magic, is your body and the bodies of many others being placed into the ground? What happened to you?"

"Our people, your ancestors, have experienced much of the Shadow. Our lands have been taken over and many of our peoples have been consumed by the greed of men. We lost our lives fighting to protect these sacred lands and traditions, yet my spirit is now carried through the jaguar. I have been preparing the path for you to come behind me and discover your truth. We have endured much pain, but that is not your destiny. Cacao is the medicine of our people, and you have remembered your role in its resurrection."

"Cacao is from our people but it is for all! I remember loving chocolate my whole life. The first time I had cacao is also when you told me that my ancestors were calling and to remember! So if my destiny is not of this pain like my ancestors, then what is it?" Lana asked.

"Your destiny has been and is currently being fulfilled. You are already the answers to the prayers of your ancestors. By your life, you fulfill the dreams of all those you now see in front of you. Your whole life you have turned the mundane into the magical. As your Father, it has been my purpose to use all of my energy in preparation of you living out your destiny. You are here to abundantly share the remembrance of what we all seek, what we all feel, what we all desire; to love freely and be fully loved in return," the Jaguar said. "Now dear child, walk freely amongst your ancestors, harness the power of these sacred lands, and celebrate with ceremony in the temples of your people. What you see around you is also found within you. Stay in your heart and remember, I am always watching over you just like our mother, Pachamama is always here for you. Keep reaching up to me through Father Sky and remain grounded into Mother Earth. You have returned in perfect, divine timing. And Lana, I always looked forward to the chance to tell you that I love you."

They gazed lovingly at one another and the Jaguar nuzzled her softly, filling her up with love. Lana looked deep into his golden eyes and he basked in her golden light, and they felt a divine love that they had both searched for their whole lives. She was imprinted with his spirit, and their souls intertwined. The bond was sealed, and the Jaguars' purpose was fulfilled.

He walked into the midst of the ancestors and as he moved through the temples, his spirit dissipated into the star-studded sky. Lana forgave him as he left, knowing she could remain connected to him through her own remembrance. In full liberation and humble recognition, she moved with grace through the landscape surrounding her. Taking part in ancient rituals, sipping cacao in ceremony, learning from her ancestors, and fully feeling like her truest self,

Lana absorbed all that she was able. As she explored these ancient lands, she heard a song that permeated the entire land. Pachamama sang:

"No longer can you deny my voice.

Now is the time to align and connect.

In the present moment, we can rejoice.

Reach out to me.

Remain open and feel my presence.

I have always been here holding you.

Loving you.

Waiting for you to awaken.

With your heart open, I can rejoice because my whispers were finally loud enough to shake you from your slumber.

I rejoice as you come home to yourself and I rejoice as you rise into your magic."

Speaking directly to Lana, she reassured her, *"You come from divine magic child. You remember now. And so now it is up to you to live this truth and be in your purpose, giving your magic to the world. Remember, you have the power to awaken and rise into your truth at any moment. Your destiny is one of bliss because of the pain."*

Lana spread her wings as her soul lifted into flight. Leaving the sacred site, she glided on the winds that had Pachamama sent to guide her back to the ceremony with her friends Alice and Sheila.

Lana felt her wings, and remembered she was capable of infinite possibilities. Her physical body may not have been able to fly like the birds in the sky, but she could soar with her soul and feel the expansion in her body. She was in her truth, in her power, and nothing could take away her wings.

The girls grew weary from the excitement of the ceremony, so they decided to walk back to Casa Alegria. Wishing her fairy-like friends goodnight, Lana went straight to her bungalow. Even though she was physically exhausted, she felt like she had just woken up. Wanting to speak to someone who she could trust, she called her Nana.

"Hi Nana! Can you talk? I want to talk to someone outside of this magical world I am living in because it feels like a dream. I've just had the most incredible experience of my life, and I can't go to sleep because it feels like I've finally woken from sleepwalking."

"Hello darling! Okay tell me. What happened?" said

Nana with curiosity.

"I just went to a cacao ceremony and then saw all of our Mayan ancestors," said Lana.

"Oh yes, how divine!" said Nana.

"Yes, a cacao ceremony. It was a gathering where we drank cacao. It helps us to release our fears and open up to our inner truths. It was so magical, and when my heart bloomed open, I saw myself as a child first, and then I saw my father's spirit. I now know that he always truly loved me and still loves me. It was as if he sacrificed himself in order to give me unconditional love in his own way. In his human form he didn't know how to convey his love or live his purpose. He said his intention with leaving when I was young was actually his way of giving me more love and power. He is continuing to live in my heart and live through me. Do you know what I mean?"

"I am so happy for this experience you've had Lana. That is so incredible. You deserve to know that you are fully loved. Your father always loved you in his own way." Nana paused thoughtfully, "And I am so happy you've experienced the ceremony. I've never been to a traditional ceremony, but I wish for it." Nana laughed with joy. She recognized Lana was brimming with her childlike essence, and it had been a long time since she had heard Lana speak with such excitement.

"A ceremony is the kind of thing that can't be fully explained. It has to be felt first hand, so it's hard to put into words how powerful that experience was. It feels like I'm in love, but with life and with myself. I just wish you could be here. I wish everyone could experience this," Lana exclaimed!

"I wish too," said Nana, as she coughed into the phone. "But hey, I have to go. I am so happy for you Lana. Send me pictures and videos if you can. Maybe that'll give me an idea of what it's like. I love you so much."

"Okay. I love you, too. Have a good night. Send my love to Mom," said Lana.

As Lana put the phone down, she realized that no explaining or videos could do the experience justice. This kind of occurrence had to be felt wholeheartedly. Lana knew that the cacao aided people into tapping back into their connection with their heart. She realized that her gift was to be a reminder to all how to connect to their own divine magic. She would do that by giving this kind of blissful experience to others. Her truth was to open others up to their magic with the aid of the cacao as medicine so they could live directly connected to Pachamama.

A big smile came across her face, and her eyes widened. She wiggled and jumped on her bed, hugging her hands to her heart. It was like she'd fallen in love with life and life was loving her back. She took a deep breath, closed her eyes, and prayed. She gave thanks to her ancestors, to Pachamama, and to Great Spirit for assisting her in this awakening. Feeling full of the deepest gratitude, she remembered an ancient and powerful word the Shaman used. "Maltyox!" exclaimed Lana.

Lana was inspired by cacao and filled with love. Still unable to sleep, she walked into the shared area of her new home. She found Sheila sitting and gazing at the stars in the night sky. The room was an open space without a roof, so stargazing was a common nightly ritual.

"I am still so awake and happy!" Lana said.

"I know what you mean. It's all those bliss molecules in

the cacao," said Sheila.

"I guess so," laughed Lana.

"So, what are you really doing here?" asked Sheila.

"I can't sleep."

"No. I mean here in Guatemala."

"Oh! I felt a calling from the land. I know that my ancestors are from here, and so I believe they guided me back so I could reconnect with them, with Pachamama, with my Father, and with myself," Lana said truthfully. "It feels so effortless to open up and connect here. It's all happening in divine timing. Everything up to this moment has led me here to recognize my purpose. Do you know what I mean?"

"I love that! I remember when I first arrived, I knew deep down that I needed to be here. I also connected with myself, with the land, and Mother Earth. I believed that this place would be healing for me and it really has been. That's why I haven't left," said Sheila openly.

"I can see that. I feel like it could be really easy to stay here in bliss and never look back," said Lana.

"Exactly," affirmed Sheila.

They mirrored the same smiling faces back at each other

and Lana felt like she was talking to Juniper or Marigold. She was so grateful to have finally found human friends as lovely as her childhood ones.

"Well, I'm off to bed. I think tonight warrants some writing in my journal before I rest. Have a good night," said Lana, sighing happily as she got up to leave.

"Sleep well, dear one," said Sheila.

Lana glided over to her room and opened up her journal to write:

I love it here, and so I understand why so many peaceful souls want to stay here forever. But deep down, I know that isn't for me. I must be courageous and share this magic with people who are still searching. I must share my purpose with others just like my father shared his with me.

I know I came for a reason. I feel like I have fallen back in love with me so that I can share from this generous place. Maybe the point isn't to fall in love with someone and just procreate. Perhaps that's a byproduct from the inner magic and this innate love of life within us all. So joy is found in falling back in love with our truth so we can live in love, accepting all that comes.

I know that I am fully prepared to share this experience with others! I will make a difference in this world by living in my truth and bringing people back to their magic and connection with Pachamama.

She knew that this would be a difficult task but a worthy undertaking. She fell asleep as soon as she turned the lights off and laid on the bed. Dreaming of cacao and remembering her ancestors gathered in the temples, Lana saw the life that was possible when people returned home to themselves by living through their heart. The next morning, she woke with a sweet taste in her mouth and an enduring warmth in her heart.

Found at the Water's Edge

Lana became comfortable living in the village, and so a couple of months went by in a flash. She fit right in, working part-time at a small café to cover the expenses of her simplified lifestyle. She didn't need much to live in gratitude. She was content to eat healthy, learn from the locals, and attend ceremonies throughout the week. Lana's favorite pastime was visiting ancient ruins where she imagined cacao and other gentle herbs being prepared by her ancestors. She envisioned shamans in traditional attire performing fire ceremonies with many medicine women gathering and preparing herbs, including cacao, for use. As they prepared the cacao, the entire space smelled of earthy and delicious chocolatey magic. Lana noted how there was cacao from different areas, each one unique yet all grown naturally with their own distinct flavors.

Aglow with excitement and adoration, Lana buzzed from the cacao. Her senses were kicked into overdrive. She absorbed the fragrance of the cacao, tasting each one she was offered. She danced freely among her ancestors, learning as much about the land as she could. The reimagined ancient city was alive with magic allowing her to experience a time where her people knew the power of this plant medicine.

She had a mission of magic to share with the world, but for now the world could wait. The land of her ancestors loved her, and she loved it back. Living in remembrance of her people and in reverence to the land made it hard to leave. She sat with all the different types of cacao, taking her time to develop a plan for when she returned to the world of forgetfulness.

In the meantime, Lana established a consistent practice of movement, meditation, and ceremony with herself, using what she learned at her retreat with Sunny. Going down to the water's edge, Lana closed each day with a prayer of gratitude and remembrance. She loved watching the sky shift from a full rainbow of colors, into deep darkness with only the stars shining through. When she tried to comprehend the vastness of outer space, she felt a deep feeling of awareness and expansion from within. Staring in awe, feeling into this feeling, and breathing deeply brought Lana into her natural state of being. She felt curious like a child, yet calmed by the wisdom of her blossoming womanhood.

One day after work at the café, Lana went to the lake alone, sitting in reverent silence. She meditated by watching the water glisten in the sun. As she sat, she felt a presence near her. A tan and handsome man swam out of the water and began to walk along the water's edge. He looked a bit lost in thought, yet when he looked up and locked eyes with Lana, it was as if he had been found. As though they had both been seen for the first time by another human being, a deep feeling of remembrance washed over them. There was an instant and enduring connection through their gaze even though they had just seen each other.

"Oh hello! I'm sorry if I disturbed you, I didn't see you there earlier," said the man tenderly.

"The water and land is for everyone. I'm Lana. What's your name?"

The man introduced himself as Max. He was a writer and was in the area for inspiration for his upcoming work and visiting with a couple of friends. He was the type of man who looked serious from afar, yet once he spoke, he instantly warmed the soul with his soft and sturdy demeanor. And just like that, Lana's heart beat in a way in which to say, "Oh there you are." She was meant to be in that exact spot to meet this man, to be loved by him and love him; and so it was.

Lana and Max spent the rest of the day together, getting to know each other on a human level and intensely bonding on a deeper level. They were both from the same city in California, and yet, they had ventured to that exact place to find each other at that exact time. When they ran out of words, their souls would dance above them as they celebrated their union. There was a knowing that was felt beyond words. Sharing with open hearts, they both recognized this was what a divine union felt like.

His presence was so warm and he felt like home to her, a feeling Lana always wished was possible. Lana didn't know that a person could make her feel so safe, but he did. He spoke softly, slowly, and thoughtfully. Everything about his demeanor helped Lana to feel at peace. He exemplified being a peaceful warrior, which inspired her. He was brilliant and determined, yet kind and humble. After spending the whole afternoon connecting, Lana gave him a hug. Max blushed from the loving embrace and the scent of her naturally sweet fragrance.

The two were inseparable from then on. When Max's friends left to visit other parts of the country, he stayed with Lana. They both recognized that this was the beginning of their journey together. They hadn't talked much about their future, but he knew he would follow her anywhere she wanted to go. With his talent and capability, he could create freely from anywhere in the world. Until they needed to talk about specific plans, they lived in the moment and loved each other tenderly.

Challenged

Life was simply magnificent during this time as Lana and Max deepened in their union. They would spend time at the spot where they'd first met, envisioning worlds to create together. As they began to establish a life together, they inspired each other to create and play from the heart. They both were fully able to be themselves and embrace their magic. Life felt like heaven on earth. This carried on for several weeks, until one particular day, Lana wanted to share some specific plans for their future.

"I've been making a business plan that I would like to share with you after lunch," she told Max. "It's written from my heart, and I wish to read it outloud for someone other than myself to hear. Can you give me some honest and constructive feedback?" Lana asked, taking a deep breath. "But first, I'm hungry. Let's go get some nourishing food before we get into business!"

"I am here for it all! Let's go eat," Max affirmed.

When the fresh food arrived, Lana breathed in the

fragrance of it's sweet essence. It smelled fresh, zesty, and alive. She savored every bite, taking her time to consciously chew and absorb the nutrients from the meal. Max was naturally a slow eater, which served as an excellent reminder for her as well.

The plan was ready to be reviewed after they finished with lunch, but as they began to talk, Lana got a call from her mother. Rachel spoke with urgency. Nana was in the hospital and was very sick. That's all Lana needed to hear to sendt her mind into a frenzy. She felt disoriented by the news. It was clear she had to go back. She told her mother she'd be getting on the earliest flight possible and hung up the phone.

Max could feel her pain and held her hand. Tears formed, and so Lana let them go. There was no way to be prepared for any of this, but now she had to go back. It was time. Leaving her friends and their home in the village, Lana and Max flew back together, unsure of what was yet to come.

Back on the soil of her old life, she was overcome with emotions. She was overwhelmed by feeling the low vibrations that emanated from the city and it's hurried, chaotic people. On their way to the hospital, Lana asked the taxi driver to stop at the city park. Remembering the peace that comes from being connected to her truth, she wished to ground into the earth and return home to herself. She spotted a large tree that beckoned to her, and she answered it's call.

Lana sat next to the roots, and Max followed patiently. Having him by her side gave her strength, and he was grateful to support her. They became still, breathing together to return to their magic. Grounding into Mother Earth, she remembered her purpose wasn't to stay comfortable and quiet in the jungle, but to return to the chaos, sharing her magic with a world that was searching for its purpose.

She remembered that Pachamama was in the wind that embraced her body, the billowing tree that gave shade, and the ground that supported her. She was reminded that she could become still and feel, even amidst the chaos, showing through love, that the light could drive out the darkness. She could show that magic truly exists by embodying her light and connecting people to the truth. Even if it was hard, Lana knew her purpose was about to be fulfilled.

Overcoming her fear of the Shadows with love, Lana felt

her sovereignty and security return. Glowing radiantly, they continued on to the hospital feeling clear and at peace.

Lana went to Nana's room alone. "Nana! I'm here."

"Ahh, mi ninita. How are you here so quickly? It's so good to see you," said Nana with tears forming in her eyes.

"How are you? You scared me," said Lana, allowing the tears to roll down her cheeks.

"I'm going to be okay, baby. You know I'm strong," said Nana.

"I know how strong you are Nana, but pneumonia is scary. It's also okay to be scared. I came here as soon as I could to bring you my love and support. I missed you and have been wanting to give you a hug for months now," said Lana.

"I missed you, too. I was very sick, but I do feel better. Great Spirit knew it was time for you to come back, so I let your mom call you anyways," Nana proclaimed. "And knowing that you were coming back gave me strength and vitality. Now that you are here, you light up the room with your radiance. You look like you did when you were a child!" They smiled and laughed as the tightness around their hearts loosened.

"I love you so much, Nana. Thank you for seeing me," Lana said.

A peaceful feeling washed over them both as they trusted everything would work out. They embraced again, and Lana cried tears of joy because she knew she really was ready to share her light with others. And the one person she wanted to shine fully for was her mother. Knowing that the person that knew Rachel best was right in front of her, Lana opened up to her dearest Nana.

"Nana, how can it be that you can see my magic yet your own daughter, my own mom, doesn't see things the same? It is like she has been covered in fog for as long as I can remember."

"My dear, your mother was so hurt by your father leaving and his inconsistent, wild nature. She used to be so bright and blissful, just like you have been and are now. You carry the perfect medicine for your mother's heart. You both have gifts to share with each other. And you may be surprised when you see her these days! Now tell me all about your trip, the cacao, and our ancestors!" Nana said perceptively.

"It was incredible, Nana. It all brought me back home to myself. That's another reason why I'm back here in this crazy world. It all has to do with the cacao and our ancestors," said Lana. "Also, I met someone, and he's come home with me. But first, let's start from the beginning."

Lana carefully shared with Nana her plans to use ceremonial cacao and gentle ancestral herbs to assist people in opening their hearts and trusting their magic. She shared how she explored the ancient Mayan temples, connected fully to the essence of her father, saw the beauties and tragedies of their people, and also all about her newfound love with Max. As Lana spoke, Pachamama danced in the wind outside, and a hummingbird fluttered by the window. It brought a message of transformation, reminding her to see the magic even in dark places. As the winds flowed lovingly into the room, Lana was stirred deeply and felt ready to step into her purpose. She felt a surge of excitement course through her body after bonding with Nana and fully being seen in her truth.

After patiently waiting, Max was welcomed in to meet Nana. They instantly loved each other, which did not surprise

Lana, as he had that gift with everyone. He surprised Nana with flowers that he got while waiting, which led to much shared love and laughter.

Beginning Again

Due to their hasty departure from the jungle, Lana and Max decided to stay at Rachel and Nana's. While Lana was grateful to have a welcoming home to return to, she felt nervous about living there again. As soon as she went into her childhood room, great big sobs rose to the surface. Feeling so deeply, she released the puddle of emotions that were in her body without judgement. She laid in her tiny bed and Max held her as she cried herself to sleep, supported by his arms.

Slipping into a dream, Lana quickly found herself surrounded by pitch black darkness! Lucidly dreaming and remembering her past experiences, she first checked to see if she was standing on solid ground. Opening her eyes, she hoped to see the golden eyes of the Jaguar waiting for her. Instead, she saw a sliver of light that pierced through the darkness. Reaching out to touch the light, her hands landed on what felt like tree bark! Lana opened up the crack as wide as she could to see through the tree. Looking out, she saw she was in her own backyard and that their house was on fire! She remembered all of this vividly, realizing she was watching something from the past play out before her. Watching and waiting, Lana saw Rachel run outside, calling out to her and Nana to wake up! Rachel broke Lana's window and climbed into the burning house. To Lana's astonishment, Rachel was holding her as she flew out of the room with large, radiant wings. Flying to the edge of the yard, she laid Lana down and whispered softly into her ear. As Lana peered out from the sycamore, something blossomed deeply within her. With tears streaming down her cheeks, she watched Rachel and Nana walking towards her sleeping body. They both seemed to glide with such grace, making Lana wonder why she had never before seen their wings! Startled and shaken, she saw herself waking up at the edge of the yard and in that same instant, she woke up back into her own body.

Gasping, she sat up quickly and looked towards the doorway. With sleepy eyes and foggy vision, she saw a radiant figure walking to her. Lana wiped her eyes and felt a loving hand brush across her cheek. It was Max, present and there for Lana just when she needed him. Overcome with remembrance and full recognition, Lana softened into his arms and felt so loved.

Downstairs, Rachel had been preparing a full feast. She motioned for them to sit at the table and eat. It was clear she had done much work and preparation for them.

"Wow, this looks great," said Lana, inhaling the beautiful aroma.

"It's healthy and made especially for you," said Rachel.

"Thank you for this, Mom. I appreciate your thoughtfulness," Lana said, surprised and sincerely impressed.

"Yes of course. I figured I could practice more healthy cooking for a little while. Max, are you also vegan?"

"I consider myself to be plant-based. I try to eat in line with what my body needs. If it asks for fish, then I eat it mindfully and gratefully," said Max.

Lana put her hands around the plate and Max did the same. They closed their eyes as Lana blessed and gave thanks to the food for nourishing them. Rachel joined them, even though she was used to a different kind of prayer. They ate quietly, and after they finished their feast, Max kindly cleaned up and tended to the kitchen.

They sat down on the couch with warm cups of tea in hand, feeling grateful and nourished. Rachel loved having them there and wanted to share openly with Lana, but she didn't know what to discuss. It had been such a long time since Lana and Rachel had connected. Before Lana left on her soul-shifting journeys, she hadn't visited often. She claimed to be too busy to even visit for the holidays. Yet things were different now, and now she felt safe to be back. Not only was Lana different, but so was Rachel, in ways Lana was curious to discover.

"Did you have a nice talk with Nana at the hospital?" Rachel asked.

"I did! We spoke about many things and remembered so much love," said Lana.

"That's good. Nana was looking so much better after she saw you. It was like the lights turned back on," Rachel laughed.

"I'm so happy she's feeling better," said Lana, amused by her mother's accurate description. "You know what, Mom? I want to tell you some things Nana and I talked about," said Lana. "And I had a dream before dinner that warrants some serious exploration."

"Okay! I'd love to discuss anything you wish, darling," said Rachel.

"Oh, okay, thank you. I wasn't expecting you to be so open," admitted Lana. "While growing up, I never felt supported with my imagination or ideas. I wasn't sure what to expect from you." Lana thought she might receive some resistance at first, so it was a pleasant surprise that Rachel was so open. Lana continued, "When I visited Nana, she told me some of the reasons why you were so closed off to magic and never seemed to be able to see me."

"Oh, baby, I was a single parent. I really thought I was doing the best I could, but I always felt like your imagination was too big, and I didn't want it to get in the way of you growing up. But times have changed." She paused for a moment to hold back her tears. "I have changed, too. I always felt bad about the way I did many things. I used to wish I did things differently, but now I see things are working out. Yet like I said, I was a young, scared, and struggling single parent. I was hard on you, I know. I'm sorry I didn't give you the support you needed."

"It's okay, Mom. I forgive you. I know you loved me and did the best you could. I came to realize you were acting from a place of love, even though you had so many fears. I understand what that is like, too. I love you." She paused to hug her mother, encouraging her to feel deeply into forgiveness and release her tears. "Everything happens in the right way. I learned how to unconditionally love and support myself even in the midst of difficult feelings or experiences. And now, everything that comes up simply leads me back to love and away from fear. I've tapped back into my magic, which leads to even more love and so much peace."

"I appreciate you and love you to pieces. I always knew that you've had this magic inside you. I felt it was too powerful, and it scared me because it seemed uncontrollable and unpredictable. But now I can see that you were harnessing your power, and I was projecting my fears onto you. I hope you know that I fully support you just as you are. I love you. It is an honor to be your mother," Rachel said openly.

"Thank you for finally seeing me, Mom. I love you, too. And after the dream I had earlier today, I finally saw your wings. I feel like I can fully see you too," Lana exclaimed!

"You saw my wings?" Rachel was overcome with emotions and so Lana held her hands as she continued sharing.

"Yes, I did! Before dinner, I had a dream of the night that the living room caught fire. Actually on that night, we were sitting right here on this very couch, and you were telling me about my first day of school, about grades, and being a good student. That is such a powerful synchronicity, because all those things eventually led to me dismissing my magic and forgetting my wings. But now here we are again, this time talking about the exact opposite thing. Life has always seemed to work in that mysterious way for me. And so in the dream I had, I saw the house on fire and how it was actually you who carried me out of the house! As a child I believed I flew out with my own wings, but in the dream I saw how you used your motherly love to lift me through the window and safely out into the yard. And you were using your wings! Do you remember that?"

"Yes, I do! Oh my dear child. I only remembered using my wings to fly and find your father. It was so hard for me with him gone, and I had many nightmares of flying to find him. Now it makes so much sense why it troubled me when you would talk about your wings. Oh my baby, I thought I lost their magic forever. This is the best gift I have ever been given."

"That's exactly what Nana told me at the hospital! She said I carry a medicine for your heart and that we have gifts for each other. Isn't this the most wonderful thing to remember in the whole world? I love you so much. And to have Max here is such a blessing, too." Lana was in full recognition and appreciated Max for being so present and patient as they expressed so many emotions.

Beaming with a radiance Lana had never seen before,

Rachel seemed to now be the person Lana always imagined she could be. While Lana was on her path of discovery, Rachel was also opening up to her own truth. Nana told her about Lana's experience with cacao and their ancestors, which inspired Rachel to do some soul searching. It was as if Lana's expression gave her permission to finally listen to her feelings. Rachel slowed down her workload, and as she did, she began to change. She made time to attend church with Nana, began eating healthier, found a hobby in ceramics, and even danced often!

"This reminds me of something I almost forgot. And when it happened, it didn't make any sense, but now it does!" Rachel exclaimed. "As I was taking Nana to the hospital, she said that if she didn't make it back to our home, to remember the black jasper box, because a child of magic would need it. And now I don't know if that child is me or you."

Lana was fully bloomed and felt free to fully be her truest self. She felt a flower of truth that lay waiting within her, perfectly ready to shine upon her mother. "It is both of us, Mom! We are both children of magic. That is who we all are. And do you really have the box? That would be one of the most incredible things!"

"It's right where you left it my dear child. Nana said it was mine to remember yet yours to retrieve." Rachel pondered and felt those words deeply. She felt a fullness of light and pure radiance wash over her whole body. She forgot she was capable of feeling so much love after all the heartaches she had endured. Yet now she felt like she could finally rest within herself with a soft heart and still mind.

Magic out of the Mundane

"Mom, I'm so happy to share all of this with you because I'm going to open up a shop for magic, and I could really use some help." For the first time since she was a young girl, Lana was ready to fully share her dreams with her mother.

"A what?" asked Rachel.

"A magic shop! I'm going to have a beautiful space where people can open their hearts and come into their own magic," said Lana with excitement. "There is so much I have yet to tell you."

Lana explained how she was going to make change in the world for the better with the aid of movement, meditation, ancestral herbs, and especially cacao. They would create a space filled with love and pure connection where cacao was prepared with the intention to open hearts. She saw how people would benefit from having a safe place to instantly transform into their childlike selves and tap into their truths, free from judgement or expectation. The space would be perfectly cozy, inviting everyone to remember how simple it is to be in their natural state of being. Her mother listened intently and fully saw the vision Lana laid out before her.

"It all sounds so amazing! I can imagine it completely," said Rachel with admiration.

"I'm so excited, Mom! I even have a business plan, and I think it's perfect. I have it printed out here with me. Would you like to see it?" Lana asked.

Rachel retrieved her reading glasses and took her time to carefully read the plan. When she finished, she looked up slowly. "Wow. I love it. The writing is beautiful, and I think it's very dreamy. But there aren't any numbers. For a business plan, you have to have a five-year plan laid out with start up costs, cash flow, and such," her mother told her.

"I don't know the numbers, but I truly believe that when people envision the shop and understand the idea, they will support it, just like you. It's what I came here to do; it's a part of my purpose!" Lana said with passion brimming in her eyes.

"I hear you and understand that fully. I can help you add more to this epic plan, I just want you to understand that you will need numbers for the bank and investors," her mother said empathetically. "Better yet, I can help you right now if we start small. I know what the estimated numbers are for opening a new boutique for my company, so I can work with that framework. How does that sound? You're the boss!"

"Really? That sounds great! Honestly, it doesn't matter how small it starts, because once the word gets out, it will grow into something grander than we can imagine. People will want this experience from all corners of the earth. In our heart of hearts, we truly want to remember our magic, dance freely, and reconnect with nature," exclaimed Lana.

"I have some money that I have been saving up for a while now for a down payment on a bank loan. With that, we will have plenty of time to create the space, gather investors, and start on your dreams right away!" said Rachel.

Joining in on the conversation, Max added that he had been on the phone with his father who owned a construction company. Max said that they would help Lana build anything for her space right away. He also knew of a man who had very peculiar properties in the area. Most people couldn't use the buildings, yet to Max, it felt like one of them could be the haven in which all of Lana's dreams would materialize. With their craftiness and creativity, she knew it could all work out perfectly. Through love, trust, and collaboration, they opened infinite possibilities.

"Luckily, I am friends with the man who owns these properties. He tends to a lot of land, and I'm sure he fully supports the idea of having cacao around. He says the place is small and a bit unique, but it is a prime location," offered Max.

"Okay. Great. I trust you!" said Lana.

"Exactly. We got this!" affirmed Rachel.

"Yiii Chicoyyy," Lana squealed with the call of the cacao spirit. She twirled in a circle, then hugged her mother and Max tightly.

Several days later, they ventured to the place and found that it was precisely how Lana had envisioned it. It was magically warm and welcoming, and it looked like a treehouse! In the center was a large tree with many other native plants that decorated the magical space. Remembering the homes of her friends from the forest, she was inspired to make it a place that they would feel safe in. They covered the shop in beautiful string lighting, set up open spaces for movement and cozy places for recentering and placed greenery in every nook and cranny. Lana fit in as many plants as she could manage without turning it into an actual jungle! In a matter of days, the whole place smelled of cacao and freshly baked lemon poppyseed cakes.

It was a phenomenal place that was inviting for all kinds. Lana called out to her magical friends, and the fairies and Felix came and made homes in the tree. Juniper and Marigold lounged comfortably on the tree leaves, sipped nectar from the sprouting flowers, and watched over the sweet spirits entering Lana's place. At first it was mostly her magical friends and the occasional stray cat or dog that stopped in. But she was content to watch it bloom naturally, spending time decorating, planting herb gardens, and scattering flowers anywhere she could find space.

Things started off slowly, but after a few weeks, the word spread about Lana's magic shop, and it became the talk of the town. The mention of a sacred and enlightening cup of chocolate inspired many curious people to visit the place, and it was the enrichment of their lives that made them return for more. When people entered the space, they could feel its palpable and radiant energy. Stepping out of the built-up world around them and pausing to be still, they would notice that when they drank the cacao intentionally, a shift within them occurred as well. These small shifts created ripples that led to the shop of magic gaining quite the reputation.

Some gathered to connect, feeling the love that was cultivated from the magical place. Others gathered in stillness for a ceremony while others danced freely; whatever expression took form was perfect! Lana found herself enraptured in the intensity of it all, which was fulfilling and yet somewhat disorienting. It seemed like just the other day she was walking on the lands of her ancestors or taking part in her own very first ceremony. Pausing to be still amongst so much motion, Lana called out to Pachamama.

"My Earth Mother, Pachamama, will you please come into this place? All of this exists from the words you've spoken and the way you have inspired me. But now, I find myself getting dizzy. Why do I still feel this way if I've overcome the Shadows and have created such bliss?"

"All of this exists because of what you and your loved ones have become. My sacred elements and magical creatures have supported you, yet this is your creation. I am so proud of you. You have created in the material world that which had been only in the magical realms. We celebrate your life, dear child. Join us in the continual dance with the darkness. Watch, as you twirl and spin, how your shadow moves along the ground with you; a reflection of yourself that only exists because of the light. One does not overcome the Shadows. We watch them carefully to learn more about ourselves through our expression of the light. And yours, child, is of the most glorious radiance!" With a spin and a twirl, Pachamama illuminated the magical treehouse, blessing each patron, every plant, all the creatures, and especially her dearly beloved, Lana Livia.

Lana spent most of her time at the treehouse and especially enjoyed the early morning before anyone else was there. It was her sacred space and in it, she felt alive. When spending quiet time there, rather than feeling alone, she connected to her ancestors and to the Earth each day. She imagined her ancestors were present and could feel them around her, honoring the space, and drinking cacao in her shop of magic. She knew they were so proud of her for sharing this gift.

Listening to them intently, Lana poured out her heart into her journal: "Keep coming back home to yourself. These are such special days. The word about cacao has taken flight all over the world. I couldn't be more excited about the healing happening from this expansion. The love that emanates from here is a pure truth that will overflow into the world. I am grateful for such blessings and for the gift of sharing my magic with this wild, wonderful world."

She paused for a moment and placed her hand on her heart. "And I also want to remind myself to be still and listen, finding the magic within—without cacao or anything else that is outside of myself. We are all made of magic, we simply need to be still long enough to feel it deeply. When we love and trust in ourselves, we live from our soul's truths. This is a practice. I am not above anyone in this. We are all going through the human experience together. We are all connected and must continue to rise in love and gratitude. Listening to our hearts' call over and over again, we move with and through the pain and darkness that creeps in. I can trust myself to embody these truths so that others can follow and live life fully colored in magic. Making these ripples in the world, we shift out of the mundane and into the magical—fulfilling our purpose of loving and being loved in return." She brought her hands to prayer and bowed in reverence.

Suddenly the wind picked up around Lana, sending leaves fluttering up into the sky. The wind flowed over to a park, past a child and his mother playing freely. Pachamama's wind willed shivers up Lana's spine as she saw herself fully reflected.

"Listen closely to hear me calling you back home, reminding you when you forget. Life is a great, mysterious gift. Your mission is to recognize it as such, and create freely from that knowing. You are enough as you are. When you forget, breathe me in and remember that life is a gift. I will whisper always. Gently. But you must be still and listen. You are perfect love; A Child of Magic from beginning to end."

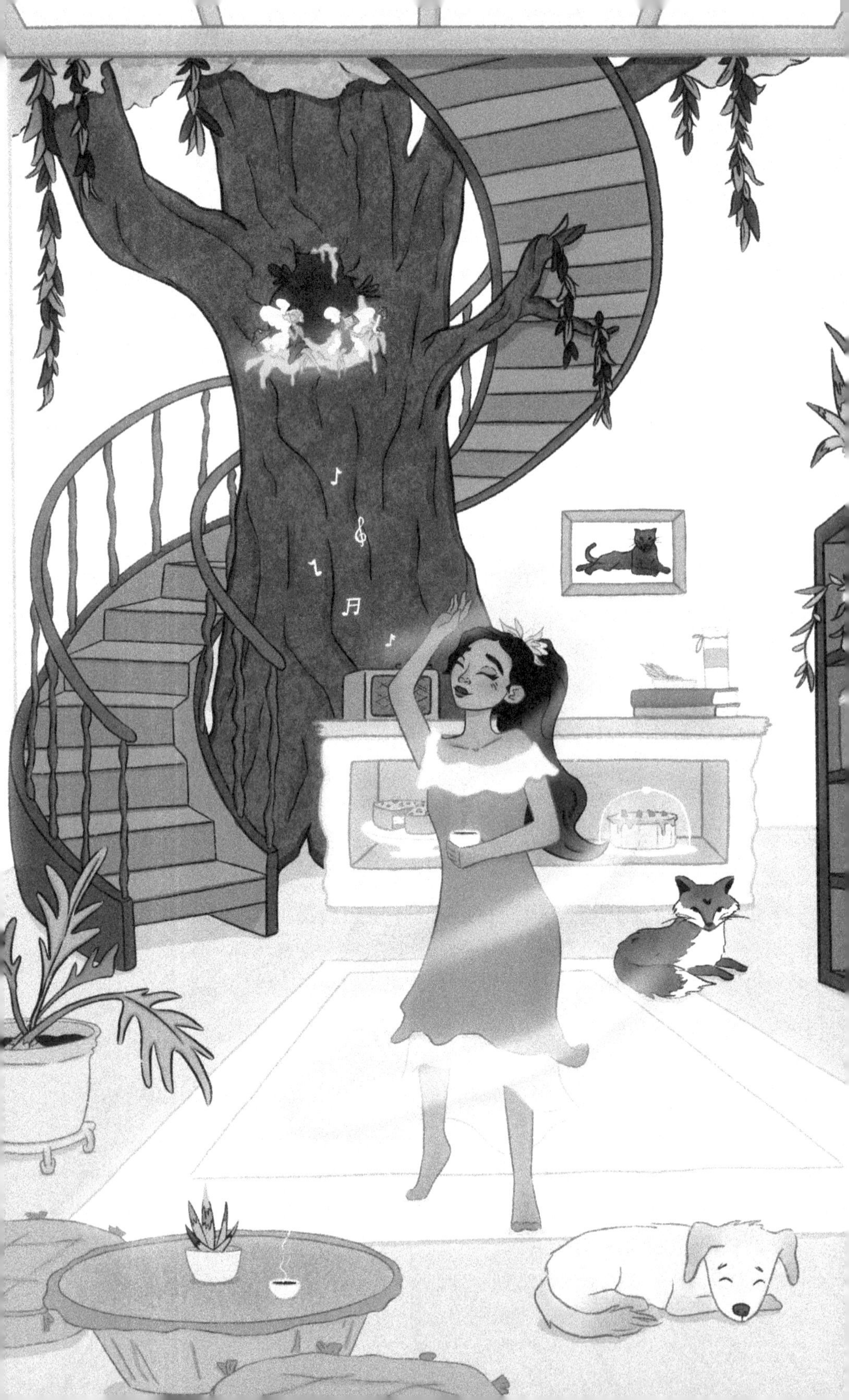

Working Within

Months passed, and as the seasons shifted, Lana felt herself changing, too. She was doing her best to find stillness amidst the chaos of the world around her, but she found it increasingly difficult. Tending to the shop each day became a chore and lost much of its magic. She noticed how occasionally she even considered giving it all up. She would fantasize about living in a forest with her beloved partner, leaving the shop behind. She hadn't shared that with anyone, but she noticed that she'd been thinking about it often. There was something about those dreams that felt destined and necessary, yet with everything going on, she didn't know how to make it happen.

One summer afternoon, Rachel and Nana decided to take Lana to a smoothie shop closeby. Lana didn't like having long, drawn-out lunches now that she was so busy. They quickly got their smoothies and were about to head back to the shop when Nana gently grabbed Lana's arm. She sat her down at a table so they could all talk.

"What's going on Lana? We can tell something's amiss. Let's talk about it," said Nana, while Rachel nodded in agreement.

With a sigh, Lana began. "You both know that I love what I've created, right? And so this doesn't always make sense, but I feel like I'm ready to let it all go. I thought my purpose was to share cacao with the world, but now I feel like my mission hasn't come full circle. Something still isn't complete. Now that the place has grown so much and people want to keep building more, I don't really even have time to figure out what's calling me away. I just can't make sense of it. I didn't have the courage to discuss it until now, so thank you for asking me."

"It's all perfect, Lana. One moment you can share a large dream with the world, and the next you can change someone's life with a smile," Rachel said, comforting Lana.

Nana could sense it was her time to speak, and she began tenderly: "My dear girls, you both are still so youthful. You have so much passion in your eyes with deep love in your hearts. From my own life, these things I know. We must live through love. However, living this way does not mean we always succeed. To truly feel complete, we must admit when we fail and fall short. By owning our imperfections we can feel at peace knowing that what we do is for love."

"Oh, yes. That makes so much sense!" Lana exclaimed. "I can see how I placed all my energy into the shop succeeding because I simply wish for all people to feel love. I focused all of my heart into work outside of myself and not within, just like I did with school when I was a little girl."

"So then ask that little girl what she wants," Rachel said. "And then do exactly that. Since you know that she is so proud of what you've created, as am I."

"Come back into balance between what you feel with your magic and what you've created in the world. Your heart knows exactly where you're being called. You are fully prepared and always supported," Nana said in closure.

Lana sat quietly with this knowing, letting it settle in before she spoke or acted on anything. She knew what was coming, but didn't know how to make it happen quite yet!

With these understandings, Lana woke the next day feeling excited but still overwhelmed. She hadn't spoken that morning. Max could sense something was taking place.

He embraced Lana and spoke softly to her. "My love, I can tell that you're feeling through something. Would you like to share what's going on?" As he spoke with loving affection, she felt it open an untouched place in her heart.

Lana sighed heavily. "Truthfully, I feel torn. I feel like I am in the middle of carrying out my purpose with the amazing place we created. Yet now another part feels like I'm done with it all, and I'm ready to slow down. I feel called to return to the forest, but I know running away won't help anything."

He understood the pressure she was under and said, "Yes, this has been intense! You just now said it yourself. We will slow it down. Actually, I have been feeling that was necessary for me as well. We both seemed to have fallen back into the trap of doing more in an attempt to become more. But we both know that's not how the heart works."

Lana smiled and nodded. "Oh yes, I guess we did. And you were feeling the same? What is it that you wish to change?" She was glowing, knowing that the conversation was perfect and everything was happening in the right timing.

"Well, we can move somewhere where we can have peace and quiet at our front doorstep. Where we can be in simplicity and live immersed in nature. We'll still be able to step back into the madness of the big city, but only when we want to. Imagine a place near a river and deep in the forest surrounded by big trees!" Smiling, Max caressed Lana's cheek.

She squealed with excitement! "Oh Max, I have been dreaming of the same thing. I can see a cottage with herb gardens, honey bees, and woodland creatures. A place to really call home, like a nest that is safe and held by the forest."

They spent the whole day feeling into their dreams. Later that evening, when she felt ready to say the words out loud, she called her mother and Nana to share precisely what she planned to do.

"I've relearned a lesson that is simply a fact of life. I created something magical, yet once again I strayed from my truth. Shifting out of my head and into my heart, these ripples of love last longer than fear. It is time I fly with my wings like an eagle and go see Pachamama in the forest.

She once gave me something that I wish to return to her; something both of you helped me to remember and retrieve," said Lana.

"We're so happy that you have gone through all of this, making so much magic in the world wherever you go," said Rachel. "You have always inspired me to be more like myself, my love."

"We love you," added Nana!

Reviving the Necklace

They found a woodland cottage nestled amongst the trees and yet still near the town Lana grew up in. The land was spacious, and the surrounding forest felt welcoming and safe. Along the back of the property intertwining oak trees grew next to a river whose trickling song could be heard throughout the home. Inside their nest, it was airy yet intimate with high ceilings, reading nooks, and sunlit alcoves perfect for cozying up and creating. It seemed specifically built for the two of them, and they loved it the moment they set eyes on it. It was an ideal place to call home, perfect for her imagination and for Max's work. Here, they could be easy and free.

After patiently setting up their home, Lana retrieved the jasper wooden box and placed it on the fireplace mantle. She knew that it contained a portal to a different time. A time where the little tokens she gathered held the highest value. A time where she didn't know anything else but to find magic in all things. To open this box was to uncover a treasure buried deep within her heart—an object that had inspired and guided her entire life. Butterflies filled her whole body as she took a deep breath, lifting the lid.

As the wooden box opened, the gifts from the forest released sweet floral aromas, reviving vivid memories of her childhood. She slowly reached in past the dried-up flowers, a photo of her parents from high school, a rusty ring that she had worn in the fourth grade, and over the shell from the mermaid until her hands landed upon the glorious necklace. Enraptured in the moment, she thoughtfully placed it back onto her neck. Resting over her heart, the magical stardust within it came to life, shining brilliantly. Full of vitality, she felt Juniper, Marigold, and Felix's omnipresence and their adoration for her transparent heart. She felt as if the child within had now become a Queen, and she remembered her divine essence once again.

Lana briskly walked outside towards the woods, gliding over to the edge of the forest. She paused to take off her shoes, opening her feet to the dewy grass and feeling it tickle between her toes. Looking up, she saw a tiny red hummingbird in the distance, and it beckoned her to follow.

She followed him with her eyes since it flew so quickly and lifted in flight to follow his shining trail of light. With a flash, he disappeared behind the largest tree in the forest. Lana landed softly on the moss at the roots of the ancient oak. Reaching out to touch the bark, she closed her eyes and sang out to her beloved Earth Mother, Pachamama.

"Pachamama."

As if her words were a password that opened a secret passageway into the world of magic, the entire forest blossomed into bioluminescent radiance! Dark green leaves transformed to reveal their colorful flowers as they danced in the breeze. The moss coating the land ignited with blue and purple hues, and the mushrooms radiated a golden glow across the forest floor. It was beautiful beyond measure—an oasis of magic and a home to the heart.

Lana gasped, holding her hands on her necklace as Pachamama laughed with a majesty that echoed throughout the forest. Hearing their mother's joy, the creatures of the forest emerged to see who had returned. The hummingbird flew over and kissed Lana on the cheek. A squirrel scampered up to Lana's feet, and a mother deer with its fawn nestled beside her.

"Hello Pachamama, it is remarkable to be here in your full presence again. You look just the same as I remember you," said Lana.

Pachamama's essence fully emerged from the tree and reached out to hold her.

"It is good that you have come back home, my child. Surely now you fully understand that the power of life has always been within you. You are the love, the magic, and the gift. I have waited for this moment in which we can celebrate the lessons you've learned and this power you've earned. Rejoicing, hand in hand, we dance once again. I am so delighted by the ways in which you have come to be yourself," sang Pachamama. As they hugged and merged into one, Lana's wings expanded, and although her physical form stayed put, her soul took flight, dancing in the sky. Lana bowed to her heart in gratitude. She felt the necklace resting on her chest and slowly took it off and laid it at the roots of her Earth Mother.

"My beloved Pachamama. I was guided by my mother and Nana to retrieve this gift. Not only has it inspired them to remember their own magic, it has revived me from the deepest of darkness and complete forgetfulness. The mystical cacao bean inside led me to remember my ancestors and find my father! Its radiance is an extension of my own magic, a magic so pure it could only come from you. I wish to return it to you and the forest so when another Child of Magic enters into this enchanted state of being, they may also receive its blessing."

"Your actions show the innocence and purity of your heart. You have come fully home to me, to yourself, and to your magic. While your offering is indeed admirable beyond measure, the magic within this forest is eternal. I therefore hold a unique and predestined gift for every single person who ventures into their own heart's remembrance. Keep the necklace as a symbol of your embodiment, and when others ask of its glory, lead them back home to me and to themselves. I will be singing, calling out to them. And for you, my child, I shall always sing a special song of praise."

The forest erupted in ecstasy, celebrating Lana as she left the sacred space, returning home to the cottage. As she skipped along, the Jaguar came along beside her. They looked at each other and nodded in utmost reverence. Juniper, Marigold, and Felix glided up next to her as well, and all together they walked to the edge of the forest. With a kiss to the fairies and a quick stroke of Felix's soft face, Lana leapt through the opening, landing back onto the dewey moss of her new backyard.

She could smell freshly baked sourdough bread and knew that Max must be preparing a delicious meal just for the two of them. She walked through the kitchen door where she saw her love stirring a bubbling pot of soup. Looking up, he saw her radiating with her natural golden hue.

"I love you! So much," said Lana melodically.

"I love you, too. Let's dance!" said Max.

Max hummed a tune while they danced around the kitchen. They shined brightly and all was perfect as it was. Lana smiled, laughing with such magnificence that all who dwelled in the forest felt her joy. Breathing in love and being in their magic, they were completely at peace. They found home eternally within themselves and with each other—free to love and be fully loved in return.

The End